SHORT STORY SSi

INTERNATIONAL

Tales by the World's Great Contemporary Writers Presented Unabridged

All selections in
Short Story International
are published full and
unabridged.

Editor
Sylvia Tankel

Associate Editor
Erik Sandberg-Diment

Contributing Editor
John Harr

Assistant Editors
Mildred Butterworth
Debbie Kaufman
Kirsten Hammerle

Art Director
Carol Anderson

Circulation Director
Nat Raboy

Production Director
Michael Jeffries

Business Manager
John O'Connor

Publisher
Sam Tankel

Volume 16, Number 93, August 1992.
Short Story International (USPS 375-970)
Copyright © by International Cultural
Exchange 1992. Printed in U.S.A. All rights
reserved. Reproduction in whole or in part
prohibited. Second class postage paid at
Great Neck, N.Y. 11022 and at additional
mailing offices. **Editorial offices: P.O. Box
405, Great Neck, N.Y. 11022.** Enclose
stamped, self-addressed envelope with
submission. One year (six issues) subscription
for U.S., U.S. possessions $24, Canada $27
(US), other countries $29 (US). Single copy
price $5.75 (US). **For subscriptions and
address changes write to *Short Story
International*, P.O. Box 405, Great
Neck, N.Y. 11022.** *Short Story
International* is published bimonthly by
International Cultural Exchange, 6 Sheffield
Road, Great Neck, N.Y. 11021. Postmaster:
please send address changes to *Short Story
International*, P.O. Box 405, Great Neck,
N.Y. 11022.

Table of Contents

Copyrights and acknowledgments

We wish to express deep thanks to the authors, publishers, translators and literary agents for their permission to publish the stories in this issue.

"Rough Red and Camembert" by Margot Titcher. Copyright Margot Titcher. "New York Bonus" by Albert Russo. Copyright Albert Russo. "A Time in the Sun" by John Rizkalla. Copyright 1992 John Rizkalla. "Polly and Pete" by John Haylock. Copyright 1992 John Haylock. "The Boss" by Janou Walcutt originally appeared in *Les Nouvelles Littéraires*. Translation by Janou Walcutt. Copyright Janou Walcutt. "The Senator's Suit" by Robert H. Brown originally appeared in *African Arts* Volume X, Number 4. Reprinted by permission of the author. "My Eyes Opened in Hackney" by Olive Winchester. Copyright 1992 Olive Winchester. "The Village Doctor" by Wale Okediran, 1992. "In Corner B" from *Renewal Time* by Es'kia Mphahlele. Published by Readers International. Copyright © Readers International. "Overbooking" by Andrés Fornells, 1992. "The Award" by Jane Elsdon appeared in *Crosscurrents*. Copyright 1990 Jane Elsdon. "American Beauty" from *Emperor of the Air* by Ethan Canin. Published by Houghton Mifflin Company. Copyright © 1988 Ethan Canin. By permission of Houghton Mifflin Company and Pan Books Ltd.

Photo credits: Ethan Canin © Lorin Kloris.

"Brain, don't falter now! Don't leave me
open-mouthed, wordless!"

Rough Red
and Camembert

BY MARGOT TITCHER

THE digits at his wrist altered from 6:39 to 6:40. The lights
showed green. Keith changed gears and moved with the sluggish
stream. He maintained a steady, one-meter distance between
his front bumper bar and the rear of the yellow Gemini ahead,
concentrating on little else in the nightly *Follow-the-Leader*.

In a bid to counteract the somniferous effect of the combination
of stale atmosphere and the monotonous stop-start motion, he
wound down the window. As he drew in deep breaths from the
chill air of the early autumn evening, his nostrils registered the
difference in temperature and the bitterly pungent smell of petrol
fumes. Vigorously, he shook his head from side to side, to clear the
warm, gray fog inside it. He tried cerebral gymnastics, attempting
to compute how many more times in the current year he
would traverse this identical route, how many journeys he had
accomplished in the previous decade, how many projected ones
between this day and the day of his retirement. By the time he

was reducing the latter problem to hours and minutes, the Gemini had widened the gap and the pantechnicon, looming in the rear vision mirror, was emitting impatient *parps,*

Touching the accelerator lightly, he resumed his place in the commuter chain. Keith deliberated whether there was, in truth, a leader at the head of the line or whether, perhaps, the links had formed up bracelet-style and were destined to travel in a blind, mindless, interminable circle.

Exhibiting his independence in the face of this unthinkable alternative, he activated the blinker defiantly and took up the left-hand lane preparatory to swinging into a tree-lined side street.

Lord, he was tired! Age was catching up with him. It was as if, with the passing of a single day, he had aged twelve months. The homeward trip depleted his reserves more on each occasion he undertook it. His sole objective: the door of his suburban, cream-brick triple-front. A simple enough goal, it would seem, yet one which was becoming progressively difficult to attain and not, by any means, to be taken for granted.

Keith navigated the well-known crescents and streets, the avenues guarded by sentinels in russet and gold. Weaving to right and left in wide arcs, enjoying the freedom of the empty carriageways, he left the crowded highway far behind. Emitting a curious glow, the long thin body of vehicles, exhaling smog, crawled laboriously away, up into the nearby hills along a serpentine path.

He nosed the Valiant out of Scenic Drive and down the steep incline of the valley road. The scent of eucalypts hung heavily in the air, mingling with the odors of cooking. Steak and kidney pudding. Sausages and mash. Curry. Keith fancied he could identify each dish. As he glided into his own driveway, the tension started to ebb, the thrumming headache—a legacy from the traffic's din—lessened and he felt more at ease, but the debilitating tiredness persisted.

However, he knew of old, that ten minutes with shoes off, feet up, a comfortable chair and a cold beer would rejuvenate him sufficiently to do justice to Winsome's evening meal. Almost before he twisted the key in the lock, he was undoing his tie, shucking off his suit coat and discarding his shoes.

Resolved not to vent his weariness and despondency on Winsome, he executed one of his party-trick, "never-fails-to-lay-em-in-the-aisle" impressions. With shoes in hand, coat trailing behind him on the floor, Keith staggered through the doorway, sank to his knees and proceeded to drag himself across the carpet.

To the grossly exaggerated "man dying of thirst" routine he brought realism with raspy croaks of "Water! Water!" then added an individual touch.

"If you have no water, beer'll do. Beer! Beer!"

On reaching his favorite lounge chair, he collapsed into its out-stretched arms.

"Boy, am I whacked!

"Win!...Win?"

The anticipated amused reaction, the greeting, was not forthcoming. The kitchen, usually the hub of all activity at this hour, was only dimly lit and silence pervaded the house.

Having staged such an elaborate entrance for the benefit of a non-existent audience, Keith felt particularly foolish. Embarrassed, he slipped into his shoes, put his coat neatly in the crook of his elbow and headed in the direction of the master bedroom.

Instead of the smell of meat gently frying, and of new potatoes and minted peas on the boil, which he had fondly conjured up on his way home, there were drifts of Imprevu and face powder.

Winsome flashed a welcoming grin over one shoulder and returned to easing a stocking up a shapely thigh. Her partly-clad flesh failed to arouse any response in him. Not that she was no longer appealing, in spite of the additional kilograms gained with maturity: maturity brought in its train the twin bonuses of self-assurance and expertise. But, awash with fatigue, his whole being was one great numbness.

He walked by Winsome and flopped onto the bed, letting his frame sink into the continental quilt, his shoes fall to the floor; and relinquishing his grasp on the jacket, left it lying crumpled beside him.

It was all of five minutes before the import of her half-guilty, half-concerned smile registered on his consciousness. The brain, as limp as the body, was disinclined to function, being more disposed toward a total shutdown than to adding two to two.

First rubbing both eye sockets with the heels of his hands, he then propped himself up on an elbow and took in the scene.

Wife, semi-dressed; Sunday-go-to-Meeting make-up on; perfume and no cooking odors, despits the lateness of the hour.

"Oh, no! Don't tell me! Let me guess!"

With thumb and forefinger he pinched the bridge of his nose between tightly closed eyes, lines of concentration striping his forehead—or was it pain?

"Something I've forgotten. A dinner? A ball? Break it to me gently, honey. Not another wine tasting? That's it, isn't it? A wine tasting! Oh, Lord! That's just about all I need tonight!"

"I'm sorry, dear. I did mention it to you yesterday. You couldn't have been listening."

The woman moved swiftly to the bed, closing the space between them with easy, lithe strides. She knelt and, looking at him very directly, spoke earnestly.

"Why don't I phone Gloria and say we can't make it? Say that something unforeseen has happened. She'll be disappointed, I know, because she had trouble getting the numbers up and she's arranged for Doctor Whiffen to give the talk, but I'll try to sound convincing."

While she was speaking, her fingers stretched out, ruffled his thinning hair and lingered to massage his scalp tenderly.

Keith rallied enough to grip her forearm and draw her into an embrace with playful suddenness. The gasp of surprise, when she found herself unbalanced, gave way to a laugh of relief as they tumbled on the bed.

"Really Keith, I mean it. If you'd rather, I'll ring Gloria."

"No, we can't let the side down, can we? No show without Punch, and all that," he added, with feigned cheerfulness. "Besides, what a waste of paint and perfume. And all those hours it has taken to make you presentable," he teased.

Throughout his undressing, Keith successfully sustained the lighthearted banter. But the pale drawn face he lifted to the water which gushed from the shower-rose, and the droop of shoulders and knees as the warmth flowed over them, told another story. He leaned his full weight against the wet tiles, grateful for the concealment afforded by frosted glass and the envelope of steam, eyes shut against tears of weakness.

Within the hour, they were standing on the porch of Gloria's brilliantly lighted pseudo-Tudor villa, pressing the two-note door chime and being ushered into the spacious over-decorated front room. Keith weathered the waves of falsetto effusiveness and extravagant affection; he adroitly steered himself past a puckering of glossy mouths and the clutch of be-ringed hands, to beach himself in what he hoped was isolation, on an island of corduroy and cushions.

The vast armchair proved less comfortable than it promised, allowing him to subside far into its depths, leaving his knees at an acute angle level with his chest. There was, nevertheless, compensation in that it was situated in a corner of the room where scarcely any light penetrated. With any sort of luck, he would be little noticed or, better yet, totally ignored as befitted his mood.

Doctor Whiffen's address on the virtues of such and such a vintage, as opposed to another, was liberally spiked with terminology intelligible only to the initiated, and received by a hushed, respectful audience. In the interests of politeness, Keith battled to keep his eyelids apart. To follow the thread of the doctor's technical discourse was an impossibility for him. He could but pray that should anyone glance in his direction he, or she, might be misled by the mask of attentiveness into which he had arranged his features and be unable to detect, through the slits, the glazed eyes beneath.

As the monologue came to a halt the guests, acting under instructions, rose from their positions as one to sample the proffered glasses of wine. Red rows and white rows, ranged behind labels of yellow cardboard indicating type and price. On a side table stood the inevitable array of dry biscuits, dips and platters of cheese.

His taste in wine being distinctly plebian, Keith joined the nearest queue careless of its objective. He had been slow to struggle upright from the cushiony clasp of corduroy and it had required a weary stretch or two, arms extended above his head, to convince his muscles they were capable of functioning and to unlock the stiffened knees. As a consequence, by the time he approached the wine table, the majority of the people were already returning to their seats, drink in one hand, plate balancing unsteadily in the other.

It was then he caught sight of her in the neighboring queue, lined up to test one of the red wines.

The moment crystallized. It was as if all movement stilled—all sound ceased. Time froze, then commenced a frenzied somersaulting action as it hurtled backwards through the space of seventeen years. Unhesitatingly, he stepped from his spot to take up the one immediately behind her, as though it were the most natural thing to do.

Frequently, throughout the intervening years, he had devoted time to fantasizing this meeting, debating how he would behave, what words he would use. He had even given some thought as to how he could contrive just such a situation. Now here, quite unexpectedly, events without a nudge of any kind on his part, had brought them close to one another, leaving him unmarked by the stain of guilt, an ingenuous mortal controlled by the gods. Both his seventeen-year-old promise, and also his obligation to Winsome, remained inviolate.

For all the conjecture and mental rehearsals, when the moment eventuated his reactions were instinctive, dependent on no stage direction nor choreography.

All of a sudden his languor dissipated, his body became alert, subject once more to the old awareness, the instant magnetism which he and Marguerite had always shared and often remarked upon.

Although the elegant head on its slender neck did not turn, he guessed she would be feeling the same as he. What was it she used to say? "In a crowded room I can see only you." And so it was for him, even now. The eminent medico, the charity matrons, the wine buffs, Winsome, were as naught—a smoky blurr, a high-pitched buzz. Reality was the slim form before him. So near he could touch her. Dare he lean forward, whisper her name,

"Marguerite, Little Flower!" and blow warm breath across her cheek, or taking the fine shoulders in his large hands turn her gently to face him?

There was a time when to tilt the small chin and kiss the upturned lips was second nature to him, as would have been the curling of her arms about his neck, and the answering pressure of her mouth, to Marguerite.

She took a step towards the table of wines, her body moving well underneath the silver-gray silk. Strange, the gift she had for wearing the apparel most appropriate to the occasion. Somehow, she made it appear that every other female in the room had put either too much effort into her dressing, or too little.

Keith was both surprised and saddened to perceive the same silver-gray reflected in the strands of her hair: Little Flower, we've lost so many years! I wonder, are you sorry, now?

A sense of urgency, a sharp fear, a quickening of his breath. Think, man, think! Do something! Say something! Lest she select a drink, return to the side of some man or other, and be lost within seconds of this rediscovery.

Not waiting for his turn, in his frantic haste Keith found himself standing level with Marguerite at the table's edge and reaching out for a glass, slopping its ruby contents down the stem and on to the white starched cloth.

What to say? What to say? *Little Flower, have you the slightest idea how much I've missed you? Darling, what are you thinking? How do you feel when you see me?* He could hardly say this within earshot of a throng of onlookers. To a smart, worldly woman who might prefer not to notice him?

A man was speaking in a thin, strained voice: "Hello, Marguerite! Enjoying yourself? What do you think of the red?"

Lowering the glass, lips shiny with the red fluid, she pivoted on her high, patent leather heels and fastened him with her violet eyes. Eyes which danced, as she held his gaze in an old familiar game, the damp mouth smiling.

"Haven't formed an opinion, yet. What do you think?" The tone calm, poised.

What had he expected? What else could they do but exchange

socially accepted banalities? Keith searched her countenance, in particular the expression in her eyes. He searched for a sign and saw nothing. Her words he repeated in his mind, eager to discern a hidden message, some indication of a secret in common, and found nothing.

Brain, don't falter now! Don't leave me open-mouthed, wordless! There must be an answer he could make. Some remark, if not meaningful or charged with wit, at least courteous and not totally devoid of sense.

He ransacked his memory resurrecting previous scenes from the protracted series of wine tastings.

The unrecognizable male voice, which he had realized must be his own, spoke again.

"I'd say..."

The wine trickled down the length of his throat, He tasted not one drop.

"I'd say...it was a bit on the rough side."

They both laughed as though he had uttered something inordinately humorous, then she turned away, striding purposefully across the room to join a tall man who was leaning against the stereo unit, watching them. Of course, the globe-trotting fiancé of seventeen years ago.

After downing his drink and hurriedly chasing it with a second, Keith sought out his wife. Winsome anxiously examined her husband's color and promptly suggested that they make a premature departure. She apologized first to the hostess and then profusely to Keith for having prevailed upon him to attend.

In the midst of her continuous string of apologies, Keith began to experience annoyance with her, an annoyance which expanded into an anger—intense and unreasoned—and a powerful desire to stop her mouth and thus halt her words. Instead, he smiled lamely at Gloria and permitted Winsome to steer him from the room.

Marguerite answered the telephone, raising the receiver awkwardly between thumb and forefinger, mindful of her tacky, freshly-varnished nails. As soon as she identified the voice of the caller, she reclined full-length along the green brocade of the ornate motel divan, settled her slippered feet comfortably on the arm rest and commenced to blow softly at the scarlet fingertips.

Only partly listening, she relied on certain key words to convey the gist of the conversation.

"...and how long are you planning to stay in Melbourne while you are down here for the conference? Long enough, I hope, for us to see you both...catch up on all your news...talk over old times. How about joining us Friday night? We're giving a wine tasting...sure to be others that you know. I have the guest list right beside the phone. Let me see...the Johnstons. You'll remember him. He's big in furniture...antiques and such. Cecily Charlton, Keith Southern and his wife. No, you won't know them...but here we are—the Ritchie sisters. It must be years since you've seen them. Grace was married...divorced...Faith is living with some chap who owns a restaurant..."

Marguerite let the gossipy prattle run on. Keith! Keith Southern! Dare she go? She had not expected to lay eyes on him again in her lifetime. Certainly, they had parted as a result of her insistence, but just to be able to see him one more time, fleetingly. To gauge what the years had wrought and to ascertain for herself that he was indeed all right. To be granted a few moments speech with him in order to say something telling, something memorable, something of great import that he could carry away with him to mull over quietly alone. To exchange sentiments so pregnant with assurance and affection that there could remain no doubt, in either mind, that the past had lost not a whit of its tenderness or significance with the passage of time.

Excuses kept occurring to her, some spontaneous, most intentionally invoked, bolstering the conviction that for her to accept this tempting offer was a logical, even a sensible, course of action. The technique was less successful than it used to be and wavering, a trifle guilty, she opted for an alternate tack. Supposing she left the decision to Leonard? He would have to be told, in any event, so let the responsibility rest with him.

"Well, thanks Gloria," she said, trusting her statement was being inserted in an appropriate pause and not between syllables. "If it fits in with Leonard's schedule, I'd love to come. Ring you back, this evening."

It would be questionable which demanded the superior skill: determining which of the three outfits, purchased that day from Georges, was the most flattering; or preventing her features from adopting a readily interpretable expression when she spoke to her husband.

Surrounded by a miscellany of belts, shoes, jewelry and petticoats, Marguerite spun around, startled, when Leonard unlocked the door of the motel suite.

She blurted out, "Gloria Soames called to suggest we drop in to a wine tasting at her place on Friday. It's only fair to tell you, before we reply, that Keith Southern will be there." Too fast—a nervous gabble. What price sophistication and composure?

Leonard plucked at the knot in his expensive wool tie until it loosened.

Impossible to measure his reaction. Studiedly controlled or genuinely matter-of-fact?

"It's immaterial to me, darling. Whatever you want."

Marguerite suspected she was being tested and knew, as she hastened to the telephone, that if this were so, she had failed.

Born in Victoria, in 1933, Margot Titcher taught primary school until her marriage. She has been writing since 1973 and her stories have been published in Australia, New Zealand and the USA. "The Letter," which appeared in SSI No. 84, brought her a prize in the Nambucca Heads Bicentennial Literary Competition in 1988. She has garnered prizes in several short story contests in Australia and one in New Zealand. Genealogical research and photography are among her prime interests.

"Was that a nightmare, or did it really happen?"

New York Bonus

BY ALBERT RUSSO

GLADYS felt radiant on this late summer evening, strolling through Central Park. It was her fifth day in Manhattan and she'd seen a lot of the city already, discovering its museums, going to Broadway shows, visiting Wall Street and the Village. She dared to take the subway a couple times at noon, but mainly she traveled by bus and on foot. She marveled at the diversity the metropolis offered, at its stark contrasts, from posh Fifth Avenue to the seedy atmosphere of the Bowery.

The only organized tour she took was to Harlem and the Cloisters. She'd heard and read a great deal about the dangers of New York City. In the Lower East Side she did come across a few drunkards, cussing hobos and drug addicts, but accepted them as part of the city's folklore. Though she never ventured in the so-called hot spots after sunset, she was surprised to find how communicative and helpful New Yorkers could be. Even the squirrels in the Park seemed to beckon her with the greeting, "Welcome to the Big Apple, stranger." Yet, amid the motley crowds, she very soon shed her "foreign" look and meshed with the surroundings as if she'd lived there for years.

Had she not won that lottery ticket at the Senior Citizens' Charity Dinner, Gladys would never have dreamt of leaving the perimeter of her Welsh village. And here she was, at seventy-five, awakening to a whole new gamut of emotions. "How splendidly resourceful is the human soul," she remarked to herself when a tall bulky fellow accompanied by a boxer swung the door open for her as she entered the lobby of her hotel. The man, a middle-aged black man clad in an expensive beige suit—double-breasted jacket, satin shirt and matching brogues—kept his dark glasses on and silently led Gladys into the elevator while the boxer blinked up at its master with expectant watery eyes.

"Stop fretting, Lady!" the man commanded in a stentorian voice.

Gladys' gaze instantly leapt towards the ceiling, searching for an escape, and finally settled on the floor directory. The words still vibrating against the metallic walls within which she felt trapped, Gladys stood petrified. As her breathing slackened, like that of a hibernating lizard, her mind began to brim with apocalyptic images and flash warnings that translated into newspaper captions: "Welsh septuagenarian assaulted by black mobster and his mongrel...Foreign matron mugged in hotel elevator then raped and stabbed to death..."

At this point a second order was fired, more ominous than the first one: "Sit, Lady, I said SIT!"

It appeared at once that a blizzard invaded Gladys' head, emptying it of all thoughts. Eyes glued to the floor directory which had just marked number 14, the old woman, slowly, very cautiously, slid into a crouching position. Her knuckles squeaked like a pair of absorbers that needed oiling. Reduced as she was to the state of an obedient robot, she ignored the lament of mortal flesh. "35" read her lackluster eyes.

A moment later, the now familiar voice boomed again, hoarse and ominous: "Lie down, Lady, it's an order!"

It took only seconds before Gladys stretched herself on the elevator's thick carpeting. "39" indicated the directory. Though she did not move, Gladys had the sudden and disagreeable impression that she was being immersed in a pool of sweat, or was it blood? She then perceived strange noises which grew closer and closer, like a veiled growl. She felt very wet and realized that someone or something was slobbering all over her face, more something than someone. Could it be...a dog's tongue? The elevator beeped to a halt.

The next morning Gladys found herself in a quandary and kept asking herself, "Was that a nightmare, or did it really happen? It seems impossible." As she crossed the lobby towards the reception area she noticed an envelope in her key slot.

"Here, Ma'am," the young employee said, "it's a message."

"A message?" she repeated, incredulous. "But I don't know a soul in this town."

This is what the note contained:

Dear Gladys,

I hope you don't mind me calling you by your first name. Please accept my apologies for the inconvenience my boxer Lady and I caused you yesterday in the elevator. I must confess however that never in my life have I laughed so much. So that you may forgive us both, I'd like to extend you this invitation. You are personally requested to dine this evening at the Top of the World where my jazz band performs. You cannot miss me, I am the saxophone player.

Cordially yours,

L.J.J. (Yes, the famous L.J.J.)

Albert Russo, a Belgian citizen of Anglo-Italian extraction, presently residing in Paris, France, has lived in many countries. He speaks seven languages and writes in both French and English. He writes short stories, novels, poetry and scenarios; his work is published in Continental Europe, Great Britain, India and North America. Among other awards, he has received the Prix Colette, the Concours du Grand Prix Litteraire de Bergerac, and been nominated for the Prix de la Liberté. His story "Marina Velcova and the Temptation of America" appeared in SSI No. 82.

"But instead of a rocket it was bullets, as indiscriminate as the droppings of a panicky bird."

A Time in the Sun

BY JOHN RIZKALLA

FINLEY watched the helicopter nuzzle up to the mountainside. The drone ceased, seemed to have disappeared in a sky bleached by sun. "Thirty, forty," he counted the seconds trying not to rush them, "fifty one!" The monster was overhead, panting at treetop level. Once again it fired into the cluster of empty shacks sheltering in the jungle clearing.

The bullets spurted along the tree perimeter then branched off without warning. There was a short, snickered scream from someone wounded unto death. Finlay ducked back into his foxhole. Who was it? He'd been so sure he was alone. He crouched, fearing another, a dozen others surrounding him with cocked rifles.

Finlay closed his eyes, caressed a dream: time, opportunity to stand up and signal to any goddamn pilot assing about in the sky that he was one too, that he'd bailed out unlike Mackenzie, survived two days, over thirty miles of jungle trek, trying to break into the shifting ripple of Saigon troops! He held to an unfailing sequence of himself, the stuff of newsreels, a chopper snorting over the clearing, himself racing towards the embrace of G.I. arms, tentacles sucking him inside, upward and away, secure!

When his head next surfaced though it was as if the chopper had never been. The silence hesitated, then yielded to a burst of chatter from scores of monkeys, birds. The problem remained. What to do about this hamlet? Reconnoiter? Skirt round it? He counted up to ten straw shacks leaning on flimsy wooden legs. The hot wind had swathed them, leaving no smoke, no movement of any kind.

After that last raid he could expect no mercy. If any of the villagers were still alive, they might deliver him up to the V.C. or hack him to death. The best now he could pray for was that the gunner for once had done a thorough job. He lingered, not really believing in luck any more, absorbed for a while in another interkill, that of insect with insect, pursued with relentless fury only inches from his face. He could have watched the mantis dismember its victims all day, pretended he was a boy again out fishing. The memory hurt so bad it forced him to crawl away to the edge of the trees. When he straightened up, he espied a dirt track that linked the hamlet with the exterior. He ran too quickly, and tripped over the figure lying in the grass.

Finlay's eyes snapped shut, his body fell before the blast of fire, cringed under the knife's incisure. Neither happened, just the itch of sweat idling down his face. Silence mocked him. He jerked up on one knee, then made sure to raise his arms in surrender. A cluster of flies responded by spiraling noisily over the man. He was quite dead, with bullet wounds weeping from the neck and face.

Something about the head caused Finlay to look closer. No doubt about it! The man was tonsured, the hair graying, curling at the sides, hardly Vietnamese. This man had come prepared for death in this uncompromising land, shrouded in a once white robe, with a girdle of rosary beads, complete with wooden crucifix.

"Jesus! A priest!"

Finlay, who had been an altar boy and crossed himself more often than he'd washed, was appalled by what still struck him as *sacrilege*. The chopper had done it. Yet at another time and place it might just as well have been his own careless handiwork.

His legs itched to run. But a sudden idea pegged him to the ground. Here was the chance to get rid of the jump suit, exchange it for the priest's robe. An impudent God was using the death of his own servant to help a renegade.

Finlay hoisted the body over his shoulders, staggered under it into the nearest shack. The change-over, the transformation would have to be total. Finlay experienced a moment's repulsion to slip on the dead man's soiled underpants. At least they were cooler, knee-long, loose fitting, could have come off any rice-picker. He replaced boots for sandals, his own identity tag with the discolored scapular. On an impulse he kissed the talisman for having sent the man along.

"Deliver me from the unjust and deceitful man. For you, O God, are my strength. Why have you cast me off?"

The robe breathed out the words, caused them to bubble up fresh inside Finlay's brain. He could have reeled off the rest of the responses without any bidding from a priest. Instead this one lay spread out, a side of lean and darkening meat, and about as anonymous. Or was he? Finlay went carefully through the robe, discovered layers of pockets and found himself a new identity: Jean-Marie Lecandec, Canadian, born in Quebec.

The flies, which had accompanied them inside the hut, were guzzling at the wounds, burnishing the face with black fury. Finlay had to hurry. It was worth the risk of only a few steps to dump the body in the darkest undergrowth available.

Once on the dirt track Finlay felt confident again, elated. As a priest, recognizable by the outfit, he stood a good chance of reaching safety. Among the V.C. were Catholics, tutored by the French missions. His own miracle continued when a minute later he stumbled upon a bicycle lying on its side, blocking the track. Out of the back pannier a chalice and paten had spilled. So the priest had been cycling when he'd been hit! To or away from the hamlet? Finlay searched further and discovered bread wrapped round a goat's cheese. He devoured both.

He was less sure about what to do with the red leather-bound missal and breviary, both in Latin, and lost his appetite at the sight of the communion hosts inside the tobacco tin. But he baulked at the idea of throwing the lot away. After all they were going to be as effective a weapon now as any gun he'd ever used. Slowly he pedaled, forcing himself into the pace of the landscape. Hunger had gone, fear refined into nervous excitement. By the position of the sun and shadows he decided the dirt track was taking him South, would filter him through the Mekong delta.

Countless naked feet, bicycle tires by the hundreds, thousands, had flattened the hard mud. But here and there a few stones, pebbles, tufts of obstinate grass still rebelled against providing any comfortable ride. Each hiccup shook the bicycle, his body, rattled his thoughts. Did anyone bury the enemy dead in the jungle? It was a crazy guilt like all guilt yet now he wished he had given himself a decent burial.

In death he'd begun to feel an odd kinship with Jean-Marie Lecandec. Hadn't they both forfeited wife, children, a posse of relatives in the search for some goddamned ambition? Yet for Finlay there had been, still were, moments of unexpected, unpaid for tenderness, with Rosie, one of the few self-conscious bar girls who serviced him in downtown Saigon. Suddenly he was hankering for her presence, even the pestering of her two-year-old son sired by another dead airman. If only he had bothered to learn the bell-sounding names of mother and child!

A scream of pain ripped his concentration apart. It had come from behind. Even as Finlay braked and swung round a different voice was screaming out an unintelligible, unmistakable order. Ten yards away stood the man, diminutive, gaunt, stooping a little with age, indistinguishable from any other of his race. V.C.? Weren't they all? The man raised his rifle.

He didn't fire though, just kept on jabbering as he advanced crablike, lips too fast, eyes too narrow, still too far off to read correctly. Finlay gripped the handlebars, grimaced. What language to speak? Hardly English! And he had no French. Vietnamese words, orders that snapped a shoeshine boy, a brothel doorkeeper into action, surfaced uncertainly into his mind. He had no choice but to stake everything on a single dice.

Seizing the crucifix dangling from his rosary beads, he used it as a spear to stop the V.C. in his tracks.

Finlay crossed himself solemnly, leant the bicycle against his body, joined hands, bowed his head and confessed in English: "I'm a priest."

The V.C. exploded with a further bout of jabbering, this time sweeping his rifle from side to side.

"CA-NA-DA! Jean-Marie Lecandec. LE-CAN-DEC." Finlay thumped his chest, as authoritatively as Tarzan.

Again the scream of pain, muffled this time from somewhere to the right. Finlay half turned and made out amid the foliage a youth, propped up against the base of a tree. But it was the legs, or what was left of them, mangled, blood and bones muddied, which held his gaze. He had to force his eyes up to the youth's face. The mouth hung open, lips trembling on the edge of another scream. But Finlay sensed that now with a foreigner to witness, he would probably be spared hearing it once more. Sometimes when these people died, so often without protest, he had wondered if they were not really of a different species, as much incapable of leniency as they were to demonstrate their own pain.

Finlay didn't need the older man to jab his rifle at the sky to realize the chopper had caused the havoc to the young flesh.

I'd have done the same! That's how much fear corrupts. He was tempted to confess to the two men.

The rifle butted into Finlay's stomach, expelled him from the bicycle. It fell to the ground. The youth's arms clamored for attention. The older V.C. shouted, the rifle gestured to Finlay that he must carry the wounded companion.

"I can't! I've got to get to the next village..." He'd forgotten about English in his panic to point South.

The rifle tilted downwards, the eyes fixed level at Finlay. He fired a single shot into the ground. Finlay's sandaled feet prickled from the grit. When the rifle moved up again, it came to rest between Finlay's heaving ribs.

"O.K! O.K!" He hated his broken laugh of surrender.

The youth was humming to himself, his hands moving down to his extremities, but though well within his reach too afraid to touch them. He started to cough then had to hold himself. His eyes flickered as Finlay bent over. Suddenly he cupped his hands, raised them, asking. What for? Finlay had no idea till he noticed against the grime of the chest bones, a metallic cross.

"Christ! He believes in me!"

That made Finlay even rougher than he might otherwise have been. He hoisted the wounded youth across his shoulders as if he were already a carcass. The shock knocked him out. The older V.C. rode the bicycle, one hand guiding the handlebars. The other held the rifle pointing forward to the hamlet.

Five, six miles away, across the afternoon sky, the drone of the chopper reached them. Finlay's heart quickened, tightened at the sound of the gun's stammer. Was it a trick of the wind? The next time the sound was much nearer. How long before the downsweep of bullets caught them all on this open track?

This was a different chopper. It had picked up his last signal. It was looking for Finlay. Even the V.C. on the bicycle believed it. He was pedaling now with urgency. Finlay caught the flutter of the other's panic. Despite himself he fell into a trot, bowed under his load, no different from the thousands of peasants hurrying pitter patter up and down the country.

The youth stayed unconscious, his arms flapped, beat against Finlay in mild protest. The body had become ever more loathsome, more repulsive with each step. Impossible not to see the display of mangled limbs too short to hang free. If only the youth would die! If only running faster would kill him! Finlay tried.

"No! It's the other one who matters..." A yard behind the V.C. was wheezing, exerting a thin strength on the pedals.

The chopper drifted nearer, impelled Finlay to outstrip the bicycle, to defy cries and warnings. He was within sight of the first shack when the Huey swept low, roared, sucked the wind about his legs, columned him in dust. Then it was gone, whipping him round like a top in its wake. The bicycle ran out of control, the rider battling with his front wheel. A stone jutting out sent it careening off sideways into the undergrowth.

"He's been hit! Hit!" Finlay was delighted. "I'm free!"

He was given no time to make sure. The chopper was back,

riding the trees, unleashing a first volley. Finlay scrambled up the steps of the nearest shack, using the youth as his shield. Inside they both collapsed on the floor, while bullets whistled away. Fists clenched he waited for the older V.C. to appear. Even if he didn't, would Finlay be any better off, trapped inside this flimsy shack, while a gun-happy chopper was policing the skies?

The youth lay crumpled, his stumps staining the floorboards.

"O God! I hope you're dead..." Finlay prayed.

He was aware suddenly of silence, the absence of the Huey. He stood up gingerly, looked round. He had strayed into some sort of communal kitchen or eating place, with benches, a long table to one side, cooking utensils, an oven in the corner. He found water in an earthen bowl and drained it. God, it was sour! He rushed to the iron pot to scoop out handfuls of cold, bland rice.

The explosion felled Finlay to the ground. He cowered, expecting the roof to collapse. But instead of a rocket it was bullets, as indiscriminate as the droppings of a panicky bird. Nearer this time, splintering the lower steps. Finlay cursed pilot and gunner. Masters of the sky, the two were practicing on a safe target! Any moment now they would stop teasing and blow up every shack in the hamlet.

Then he heard a new sound.

Distinct from the chatter, the breathless business of the jungle was the tread of an animal. It skirted round the shack, padded up the wooden steps. Finlay looked for a weapon and found a honed thin knife among the slicings of bamboo shoots, but even as he turned he recognized the long shadow laying hold of him.

The older V.C. blocked the doorway. The lips parted just enough for a whistle, a groan. The features were no longer impassive. Though the rifle went on pointing at Finlay the eyes blinked with incomprehension at the broken youth.

"He's only fainted. I'll dress his wounds." Finlay babbled, pleading now for his own life. "I'll make a bandage..."

He was on his knees, tearing at the hem of his robe. With the outsize strip that left his calves bare he made a pretence of swabbing the several mouths of the youth's injuries. When the limbs began to shudder, spurting out still more blood Finlay cried out in relief and horror: "See! He's still alive!"

The older V.C. hurried over, went on butting his rifle into Finlay till he'd dragged himself into a corner, clasping sides and stomach, unable to lose consciousness. Only hate sustained him, hate to replace the fear, obsequiousness he had shown these two. When he realized the knife was still with him, he felt a spurt of joy and honed his hate to be as true as the blade.

The V.C. had laid down his rifle, sat clasping the youth to his breast, nursing more than a companion. His son? Finlay's hate wavered, threatened to let him down. But slitting the skin of his fingers on the blade kept his purpose pure. He watched with cold and cunnlng eye as the older man, having no other part of himself left to give, rubbed his face against the boy's face. This was Finlay's chance. He started to crawl towards the stooped back. The knife was poised when the man's rocking revealed a large tear in the side of the smock. It bared more than flesh, it bared the rib cage and seemed to guide Finlay's eye to that space where the knife could best slip inside silently, unhindered. Yet that very nudity, that innocence hurt, accused Finlay. He found himself wishing for the ridiculous, for the area to be clothed, veiled—and missed his opportunity.

The air hummed, vibrated, shook with the demon wind. The man all but dropped the youth, picked up his rifle, ran bent double to the doorway. Finlay tried to scramble under the long table. The V.C. turned, saw the knife. He sprang up in a rage, bounded across, kicked Finlay over, pinned him down with his rifle.

"Shoot! For Christ's sake? Shoot me!"

But he didn't, and never did.

The shack wobbled, heralding the coming of the high-lord of the sky. The voice spluttered with staccato bullets. One found its man, spraying bits of bone and brain out of his forehead.

The body slid down, ready to embrace Finlay. It was the only movement, the only surprise in the stillness that followed.

"Oh, Rosie!" Finlay sobbed with joy, kicking himself free.

He pounced on the rifle. The youth was groaning, comatose, pumping blood into the floor matting, yet still unable to rid himself of life. Finlay stood over the figure, pinned the rifle to the chest. Closing his eyes he pulled the trigger. Click! His eyes snapped open as he pulled again. Click! Click! There were no bullets left. The gook had been bluffing, had gambled his last shot on the dirt track to frighten Finlay into obedience!

At the thought of his own humiliation, of so much time, so much energy, so much resolve stolen from him, a last thread that had held Finlay together, snapped. He fell to his knees, half-raised the youth, shook him till the lips quivered, the eyes slid open, registering fear, pain.

"Bastard! I was going to kill you just now, to help you! But now I'm going to leave you to die in this rat-hole alone..."

The youth sagged in his arms, surrendered body and soul. A hand had fastened on to the rosary crucifix, and before he could lay down the corpse Finlay had to wrench the fingers apart.

Outside the light was fading fast. Too late to escape. Finlay was grateful for the reprieve. He huddled by the doorway, watched the night seal him from the outside. Playing with the beads, mouthing words of comfort, he determined to keep vigil.

"Pere! Pere!" chanted the child.

The hand stroked his face. Because the sun was in his eyes he had to grope to catch the tiny fingers, so small they almost slipped out of his grasp. She was moon-faced, with straight hair, Oh, so serious until she realized how much she had startled him. Then she broke into giggles.

He hauled himself up and she fell silent. She was pointing to inside the shack. He blinked at the two corpses, buzzing with flies. A passing breese caught the stench of corruption, fleshed the air. The girl hurried forward, looked as if to touch them and Finlay cried out: "No! No!"

But she ignored him. She ran to the bench, pulled out strips of rush matting from underneath, lay them across the bodies, and gave them a semblance of dignity.

Later she brought him food, the same cold rice, and milk. He ate, drank greedily watched by the child, sitting cross-legged at his feet. He had dallied too long. Her parents, relatives, the whole hamlet was monitoring his movements from out there in the jungle. Yet while he'd slept, someone to his surprise had propped the bicycle up against the steps. When he'd eaten she gripped his hand, pulling him towards the cover of the jungle. He thought it wiser for the moment to humor the child. The greenery began to thin. Abruptly they emerged into another clearing. No, this was something different! By the darkened hush, the earth mounds, the lines of bamboo crosses he guessed he was in a cemetery!

Worse, a number of children, girls, boys, all sizes were bunched in a semi-circle round one of the mounds. The small ones, the tots, were holding hands, whispering, staring up at him with inquisitive eyes. Without warning they broke into a deafening sing-song, repeating what the girl had first said:

"Pere! Pere!"

Finlay was alarmed, scared when it ceased abruptly. Who had ordered silence? A figure, with a wisp of white beard, folded over a stick, detached itself from the group. He was clutching a box to his chest. He bowed before Finlay, and the little girl returned the bow. She screeched at the old man, the others, pointing back to the shacks. Some of the taller children ran off. Now the old man was shouting, addressing Finlay, mercifully not in French! One word though kept returning, a word his brain kept refusing to digest. Scanning the motley children edging, bumping towards him like sheep, the word "Orphelins!" began to impose an ominous significance. He hadn't stumbled on a hamlet, but an orphanage, the villagers were these children, orphans, the shacks their living and sleeping quarters. And now they were mistaking him, even the old man, for their dead priest!

But how? Then the absurdity struck Finlay. Of course! Like him, they could not distinguish one Westerner from another, were just as racially myopic! Unless—the notion was frightening—they were assuming he was Pere Lecandec's replacement?

The children had surrounded Finlay, eager to touch him, his robe, his beads, the bloodstains of two dead men. Instinctively he moved to the old man beckoning, guiding him round the mound of earth to a pit. Finlay hesitated. Had it been specially dug for him? He peered down, felt dizzy at the sight of the green jump suit frocking Pere Lecandec. A score of hands grabbed hold of him, arrested his swaying. The little girl led him to the nearby mound where he slumped, his arms resting on his knees, head down, trying to hide what couldn't be: the unsubstantial man revealed.

"I'm not Canadian..." He shook his head but no one helped him through his confession.

He raised his eyes and met only backs taut with attention. Hand-roped the children were watching across the clearing the approach of a cortege. Finlay stood up, awed in spite of himself. Two groups of pallbearers, children with faces, limbs, clothing streaked in dirt and dry blood, shuffled forward, threatening to crumple under the weight and swing of their dead.

But at most they paused, inclined before the old man. Not a word was spoken, no sorrow displayed, as if this ritual had been repeated so often no frills were required. A couple of children clambered down into the pit, held up their hands to receive and position first the older man then the youth. Only a layer of earth separated all three corpses. Finlay shifted his gaze and caught sight of the shacks through the foliage.

"What am I doing here? I should be away on the bicycle..."

The little girl bobbed her head against his hip, recalling his attention. He looked from her to the others, felt the stare of every child nailing him to his side of the grave. The old man was hobbling up, flanked by one of the tots carrying the box. He opened this, pulled out a red leather-bound book and presented it to Finlay: Pere Lecandec's missal, rescued from the bicycle.

At a signal from the old man the little girl started the chant: "Pere! Pere!" The whole assembly chorused it.

Finlay opened the book, but the Latin defeated him. But then wouldn't the words be just as meaningless to this congregation? His eyes settled on a phrase he'd heard before:

"Libera me, Domine, de morte aeterna, in die illa tremenda..." Finlay read aloud, spoke words he had always found hard to pronounce, observed beyond the page the intensity of the faces, and was moved to believe what he could not understand.

He paused for breath, overwhelmed by the gale of unbroken voices that responded. Only the numbers turned the screech into a rich harmony. The old man was waving his stick, spurring them on.

"Stop it! Stop it?" Finlay broke into a desperate yell. "I'm American! American! Your Pere Lecandec is there...in there..."

He hurled the missal down into the open grave. The heads jerked up, the voices cut out, the monkeys ceased to squabble. The echo drifted around too scared, too shocked to settle. Then inexplicably the children broke ranks, screaming as they scattered. The old man brandished his stick, lost his box, lurched after them. But no one listened to his pleas. In seconds Finlay who'd expected to be the first to leave, found himself alone, except for the little girl burying her head in his robe.

"Let go!"

Only now did he hear the hurrying of the wind, the whirring heralds of freedom. He counted three, four, five of them. They were going to skim over the hamlet.

"Let go! I've got to signal to them..."

The child clung more tightly to his leg. It flashed across Finlay's mind that if he was going to be rescued, then why not salvage one orphan from this mess! He lifted the girl, clasped her to his chest. He ran, battling through the undergrowth.

But he was not quick enough. He was beaten to the clearing. The machines bounced across, and like visiting angels did not require a second run. The blast of explosions sent him reeling to the ground. His body covered the child. In a daze he glimpsed at the shack that had sheltered him, punctured by a rocket, the roof snap open like an umbrella, then swoosh up in a shower of straw. For minutes after the choppers had said farewell, the air was choked with dust, with the incense of sprigs burning.

The girl scampered off. Coughing and spitting Finlay gave up trying to call her back. He watched the tiny shape melt into a barren landscape of smoke, and felt oddly deserted. He limped to a nearby tree, slumped down, examined the deep gash in his leg. It would need cleaning, bandaging, rest. Why hadn't they just killed him outright? But as time passed his bitterness softened as he realized there had been no casualties among the children, that he was even beginning to recognize some of them. They were on their knees, digging, scavenging among the ruins. Others were building a fire, setting up a shelter for the night. And all the time the old man hobbled around, directing them with his stick.

A bell tinkled, alerting Finlay eagerly to his feet.

"Pere! Pere!" called the happiest of voices, as the bicycle wobbled up to him. It was intact, miraculously intact!

The little girl had rescued it, was leading a whole group of children in offering it back to him. Finlay's heart tightened at so much trust, so much need. He struggled to settle her on the saddle. It was the signal for the others to form a queue, wait patiently for their turn to snatch a ride.

"Where shall we go?" He asked in bewilderment and they all burst out laughing.

Born in 1935, of an English mother and Egyptian father, John Rizkalla was taken to Cairo at two months of age. He attended Manchester University and worked several years in France and Germany. He was Head of Modern Languages at a secondary school in England when he decided to devote himself more fully to writing. His stories are published in several countries and frequently have an Egyptian setting. His story "The Black Figurine" appeared in SSI No. 71.

"I wished I could pass out until the next day when I was going back to Tokyo."

Polly and Pete

BY JOHN HAYLOCK

ABOUT two months after my arrival in Tokyo, a letter came from my sister asking me to look up an old English couple who lived at Kashikojima, a fishing port on Ago Bay near Toba in the Kii peninsular. Not far from Ise, where is situated the principal Shinto shrine of Japan, and one and a half hours by train from the industrial city of Nagoya, the place was rather remote, although Ise, for its shrine, and Toba, for its pearls, attract swarms of tourists.

The purpose of my stay in Tokyo was to make arrangements for the translation of a number of my London firm's technical books, and for a reciprocal agreement to be made for some Japanese publications. I was finding the going hard and my estimated visit of several weeks proved optimistic and had to be extended indefinitely. In order to economize I soon moved out of the hotel I first patronized and into an apartment, a tiny box of a place.

Foreigners often make the mistake in thinking that the Japanese clinch business deals in a trice. In fact, and I learnt this after many meetings that seemed to lead nowhere, they are slow in reaching an agreement, slow, thorough and painstaking, scrutinizing the smallest detail and discovering problems one hadn't thought of. But once they have decided, they move fast.

I had arrived in mid-March. Friends in London remarked how lucky I was to be visiting Japan at cherry blossom time, and I was excited about it too. However, it proved to be a cold spring and it snowed, which was something unheard of in April. The cherry trees in the little park near my flat obeyed nature and bloomed, but the branches were weighed down by snow and the blossoms quickly became ruined and fell. There were photographs in the press of the phenomenon of cherry blossoms and snow at the same time. I shivered and stayed indoors as much as possible, but the urge to pay homage to the national flower of Japan is so strong that groups actually sat under snow-laden trees, sang dirge-like songs and drank sakè. May was delightful with azalea shrubs in flower all over the place, even on the railway embankments of the surface line that circles Tokyo. I thought the colorful azalea every bit as pretty as the cherry.

Time passed. Oh dear, business was barely progressing! June, a month of rain, arrived. It was hot too, and unpleasantly humid. I have never suffered from claustrophobia, but the confined space of my quarters made me feel trapped. In an attempt to rid myself of this feeling I would go to the nearby station and patrol its vast underground concourse. The trouble was that it seethed with people rushing to catch trains, to keep appointments; it was like an ants' nest with the lid off. The Japanese only stroll when they are legitimately on holiday at a hot spring spa or a seaside resort; anyway, a station is not a place to wander about in. People kept bumping into me. I was in the way. Foreigners are often in the way in Japan.

The Japanese publishers were cordial enough. They took me to dinner, and on occasions I went drinking with them after office hours. I never got to know them. They had their own social lives to lead. Many of them lived two hours away from their work and so spent a quarter of their day in trains and buses.

I had met a few members of the foreign community and been invited to dine at some American and British homes, but I had not struck up any friendships. The Japanese rarely invite one to their homes. This is because many of them live far out of the capital, and their apartments are often so small that a foreign guest presents problems: he may not like sitting on the floor; he may not be able to eat raw fish or boiled rice; he won't speak Japanese and his hostess will not speak English; he will upset the children as they will not be able to sprawl about the floor watching television or studying.

When I got my sister's letter telling me that she had met a friend of the Crosby-Johnsons who lived in Kashikojima, I thought I might visit them. I had only once been out of Tokyo since my arrival and that was when I spent a weekend in Kyoto, the *Florence* of Japan, and a city so full of wonders that a sojourn of three months would not do them justice. In reply to my letter Polly, Mrs. Crosby-Johnson, said that she and Pete, Colonel Crosby-Johnson, would be delighted to put me up for a weekend beginning on the Friday. "Polly and Pete!" They sounded like a musical-hall turn. Coward's "Red Peppers" came to mind. Polly gave me the times of trains to Kashikojima. It was arranged that I should go down to visit them in August. I don't really enjoy staying with people now that I am approaching middle age. Being a bachelor, I have selfish ways: I like to read in the early hours if I can't sleep and a trip to the lavatory is usually necessary during the night; I like to get up slowly and late, have breakfast in my pajamas with a newspaper, and wash and dress afterwards. However, I supposed I could bear three nights with the Crosby-Johnsons.

I had been on the Shinkansen, the bullet train, before, when I went to Kyoto and this time I again traveled second class and not by green car, as first is euphemistically called. Second class is all right if one has one of the seats on the side that has two places. To be in the middle on the other side, which has three places, is not to be recommended since one is usually larger than one's Japanese neighbors and inclined to overflow into their territory. On this occasion I was relieved to have an aisle seat on the side with two places and the "*Fuji*" side too, but the revered mountain was invisible as it often is in the summer. I bought a can of beer and a box of sandwiches from a girl dressed as a prewar parlormaid. Like the other salesgirls and salesmen she, chirping out her wares, wheeled her refreshment trolley up and down the train throughout the journey.

At Nagoya, two hours from Tokyo, I changed on to a private line with the delightful name of Kinki, which in fact proved to be quite straight and not peculiar in any way. The constant announcements through the loudspeakers in the carriage were incomprehensible to me, but I didn't have to worry about when to get out as Kashikojima is at the end of the line; in any case Japanese trains are so punctual that if one knows the time of arrival one knows where one is.

Pete, Colonel Peter William Crosby-Johnson M.C., C.B.E., was immediately recognizable. He stood tall and white-haired and white moustached, by the ticket barrier. He was wearing a light blue, short-sleeved shirt, khaki shorts, dark blue stockings to his knees and well-polished brown shoes, old but well made.

I went up to him at once. "Colonel Crosby-Johnson?" I said.

"Correct. You must be Jeremy Bradshaw."

"That's right."

We shook hands.

"Is that all you've got?" he asked. He gave my brief case and grip such a disparaging glance that I wonder if he had expected me to bring my dinner jacket. Only a shirt and slacks are needed in Japan's sticky summer, unless one is on business, then a tie and a jacket are *de rigueur* though unbearable, to a Westerner at least; the Japanese don't sweat as much as Europeans. "Let's shove your bag in a locker here and go up to the hotel and wait for Polly. She's shopping."

After depositing my grip, we left the station and walked up a steepish hill to a large tourist hotel which dominated its surroundings. "Our local pub," the colonel informed me during our ascent, which I found more bothersome than he. He was lean and fit, obviously a man who had looked after himself. That was my impression. "The trouble is," he went on, it's deucedly dear."

"Everything in Japan is deucedly dear," I replied, reiterating the old-fashioned epithet.

"Except for eggs," he said. I understand they're cheaper here than in England, and so are oysters, and cars."

"Cars?"

"Yes. You can get a jolly good one, four door, for £4000. And the oysters here are top-hole. Pity they're not in season now."

We approached the hotel, a block of a place without any decoration to relieve its sharp lines; the drive, though, was bordered by small Japanese pines, their branches growing at improbable angles, and hydrangea bushes which still bore a few faded blooms. The doorman, dressed pretentiously in a pink uniform and peaked cap, saluted the colonel, who nodded in reply and led the way through the swing doors into the lobby, which was delightfully cool and commodious and had that air of specious luxury common to tourist hotels.

"It's not yet five," said the colonel, "but we might as well have a noggin while we're waiting for Polly." He went ahead across the hall, receiving a few jerks of bows from waiters, and into the bar, a large room with a bow window looking on to a lawn beyond which were shrubs and trees partly screening an inlet of Ago Bay, the main feature of Kashikojima. The colonel signaled to the barman receiving in reply a warm, *"Konnichi wa, Johnson-san."*

"We'll sit here," said the colonel, indicating a table in the window round which had three armchairs. "What's yours?"

"It's rather early for a drink, isn't it?"

"Let's make an exception, shall we?" the colonel's blue eyes sparkled like those of a boy about to do something illicit but pleasurable. "Barman-san!" he cried.

"Hi!" came the response from behind the bar.

The colonel turned to me and repeated, "What's yours?"

Remembering the remark about expense, I said, "A small beer, please."

"Right." The barman was at our side. *"O-beeru chisai, kudasai,* Takahashi-san. And *watakushi* gin tonic *irimasu, kudasai."*

"Arigato-gozai-mashita, Johnson-san," said the barman deferentially and returned to the bar to carry out the order.

"What did he say?" I asked.

"Only thank you. It's quite a mouthful in Japanese."

"You seem to manage all right in the language, Colonel."

"Oh Pete, please. We don't stand on ceremony. Manage all right? Yes, I suppose so, Jeremy. It is Jeremy, isn't it?"

"Yes."

"I used to know a Jeremy. Jeremy Bradshaw, was it?"

"My name is Bradshaw."

"Oh yes, of course. Jeremy...It's awful how one forgets names. Anyway this Jeremy—"

The drinks arrived at the same time as a large, red-faced English woman in a white skirt, a sky-blue sleeveless blouse, and a wide-brimmed straw hat. Pete and I rose.

"You've started already." There was a shade of disapproval in her pleasant, well-modulated voice.

"Polly, dear. This is Jeremy Cottrell."

"Bradshaw," I corrected. I shook hands with Mrs. Crosby-Johnson.

"I'm Polly. It's good of you to come and see us."

"What's yours, darling?"

"I don't think I want anything, Pete. And I'm driving."

"One for the road," said the colonel as if making a serious suggestion.

"A Campari soda, then," she said to the barman who was hovering by the table. The room was empty except for two Japanese men who were sitting up at the bar.

We sat down.

"Yes," murmured the colonel, reminiscing. "Jeremy Cottrell. He was a funny chap. I knew him when we were in Baghdad. I was the assistant military attaché. Jeremy was part of a training team sent out to help run an officers' school for the Iraqi army. This was in the early fifties, before the revolution and the murder of the King and the Crown Prince. I remember once in Rashid Street, which was always jammed with traffic in those days—'spect it's worse now, everything is—"

"Oh don't go on about Jeremy Cottrell, Pete. This is Jeremy Bradshaw."

"Timetable, what?"

"A bit before my time," I said.

"How was your journey, Jeremy?" asked Polly, politely, but in a way that suggested she wasn't really interested and was merely making conversation.

"Very ordinary. The Shinkansen to Nagoya, and then the Kinki line here. It seemed to be quite straight." I laughed at my feeble joke, but neither of my companions did.

"Kinki," explained the colonel, as if starting a lecture, "is short for Kintetsu or Kinki Tetsudo or the Kinki-Osaka-Kyoto Railway. Kinki is the name of this region."

"What a marvelous view!" I remarked after a pause during which I looked out of the window at the garden and the narrow creek thickly bordered by trees.

"Isn't it?" agreed Polly. "We love it here, don't we, Pete?"

"What's that?" The colonel had finished his drink and was gazing in the direction of the bar. "*Mo ippai*, Takahashi-san, *kudasai*." The colonel lifted up his glass to underline his order.

The barman brought another gin and tonic and a small beer for me as well as a bowl of peanuts and little rice biscuits, brown and lozenge-shaped.

"Well, cheers," said the colonel.

"Welcome to Kashikojima," said his wife.

"Thank you," I said. "Here's luck." I wished I had asked for a gin and tonic as I hate beer. I had only asked for the stuff because Pete had complained about the expense of the establishment, and I had presumed that he, being my host and a resident, would insist on paying.

"I had such a business parking near the supermarket," recounted Polly. "There seem to be more cars each week. When we came here fifteen years ago, one could park almost anywhere."

"When we first came to Japan in the late fifties—I was attached to the Embassy—we felt sorry for the Japanese being so poor, having to struggle. Now the boot is on the other foot. In a big way." Pete gave a hollow laugh.

"But we love it here," stressed Polly, looking out of the window. "Don't we, Pete?"

"Eh?" Pete picked the discreetly rolled-up bill out of its little glass container.

"May I look after that?" I offered.

"What? Oh no! Will you really? That is good of you." Pete smartly handed me the bill.

The drive to the Crosby-Johnsons' house was through pretty

wooded country. In addition to the dark-green trees were bright emerald rice fields and blue coves crisscrossed by wooden frames. I asked about the frames and the colonel, who was sitting in front beside his wife, turned to me in the back: "Oyster beds," he explained. "Cultured oysters, for pearls, for the table. You've heard of Mikimoto pearls? They come from around here. There's a factory at Toba up the line. You passed through there on your way here." He turned to the front and addressed Polly: "We might go there and to Ise on Sunday, darling. Cottrell ought to see Ise and the pearl factory."

"Yes, darling." She turned into a side road, drove down a slope and then up a steep hill and there was the house standing alone among pines on the left side of the road. A concrete box of a house which, except for its sliding windows might have been on the south coast of England. The views on to Ago Bay and its inlets were spectacular.

Pete alighted and took two plastic shopping bags and my grip out of the boot, while Polly went ahead and opened the front door.

I picked up my grip, which Pete put on the ground. "What a lovely view!" I said looking at an inlet of the Bay. "And what wonderful air!"

"Filtered by the pines," explained the colonel. "Better than that dirty polluted muck you've been breathing in Tokyo."

The house—did they regard it as their *dream home?*—was ordinary and, apart from the sliding windows, was not very Japanese. Downstairs were the kitchen, the living room, which had a bar, Pete's den and a bathroom. The pines grew close to the house and from the living room window there was a view of trunks of pines and through them glittered a creek. The stairs were ladderlike. My room was next to Polly's and Pete's. There was a lavatory too on the first floor. "Useful, if you want to pump ship in the night," the colonel said. "I have to nowadays."

Although there was no house near, the bedroom windows were of frosted glass like the windows in Japanese town houses and flats. I presumed the builder was accustomed to putting in frosted glass and never thought otherwise. The Japanese are slaves to convention.

"Come down when you're ready," said Pete. "We'll have a noggin before dinner. Dinner's at half past seven. No need to dress." The last sentence was uttered without a hint of humor. Did he really think that I would change, and into what? I unpacked my few things and went downstairs with the bottle of Scotch I had brought as a present. Pete was sitting in a winged armchair by the fireplace, obviously *his* chair.

He lowered the *Japan Times* as I descended the last stair into the sitting room and looked over the top of his half-moon spectacles. His eyes lit up when he noticed the bottle I was holding.

"I've brought this for you."

"That's very good of you, old chap. Many thanks."

Pete had a glass of what looked like whisky and soda on the table by his chair. "What's yours? Beer, isn't it? Hey, Polly! Pol-*lee!*"

"Yes?" She shouted, sounding irritated.

"Beer for Cottrell!"

"I'd rather have whisky, if you don't mind." I was still holding the bottle. Pete didn't seem to hear. He had raised his newspaper. There was an entrance into the bar from the kitchen and through it came Polly with a small bottle of beer. There was no way into the sitting room from the bar, no part of the counter lifted up to allow access, so Polly put the bottle of beer on the counter with a glass, facetiously saying, "'Ere you are, sir." It was about the only time she made an attempt to be humorous.

"Thanks." I put my bottle of whisky on the counter. "I've brought this."

"That is kind of you." She placed the bottle on a shelf beside other bottles, most of which were empty or nearly so. She was about to return to the kitchen when her husband cried out, "Polly, the other half." I looked round. Pete was holding up his empty glass. "Do you mind?" Polly said to me. Realizing that for Polly to come into the sitting room from the bar meant her going back into the kitchen and crossing the hall before gaining the presence of her master, I went over to the colonel and ferried his glass to the counter.

Pete gave a grunt when I put his fresh glass of whisky and

soda on to the table by his chair and went on reading his newspaper. I sat on the sofa, which faced a television set in the hearth. Opposite the colonel's chair on the other side of the fireplace was another armchair, clearly *hers*. Apart from the bar the room was like many an English sitting room. In front of the window facing the creek was an escritoire on which were photographs, and in the corner between the two windows was a bookcase on top of which were some pottery vases. On the mantelpiece above the television set was a Victorian carriage clock flanked by two blue and white Imari vases, bulbous with long necks. The vases made the clock look out of place and vice versa. Above the mantelpiece was a three-quarters length oil portrait of Second-Lieutenant Peter William Crosby-Johnson in dress uniform. Over the bookcase hung a Hiroshige woodblock print, one of the stations on the Tokaido, it looked like. I wondered if it were genuine. The clock gently struck seven. Pete turned on the standard lamp by his side and invited me to turn on the one between the sofa and Polly's chair.

"You don't want that thing on, do you?" asked Pete, waving a hand at the television set. "There is news on now, but we usually look at the nine o'clock bulletin on NHK." He went on reading the *Japan Times*. I wished I had brought downstairs the book I was reading. I wished I had insisted on having a whisky. I wished that my sister had not asked me to look up these people.

Polly appeared behind the bar and laid two places on the sitting room side of it and one on her side. "Another beer, Jeremy?"

"Might I have a whisky instead?" I rose. I could feel the colonel's eyes upon me as I went up to the bar.

"Which whisky would you like?" Polly turned towards the shelves, whose empty bottles outnumbered the full ones. "Japanese or Scotch? Pete drinks Japanese, Suntory *kaku bin*, the square bottle. Would you like some of that or some of the whisky you brought?"

"I'll have one for the road," cried Pete.

"You've had your two, dear."

"One for the road, please," called out the colonel, peremptorily. "Cottrell, do you mind?"

I turned. The old man was holding up his glass. Taking it, I said irritably, "My name is Jeremy Bradshaw."

"Oh yes, Bradshaw, Jeremy. Timetables. You remind me of Jeremy Cottrell. He was in the training mission in Baghdad."

I took his glass and mine up to the bar.

"Well what is it to be, Jeremy, Scotch or Suntory?"

"Scotch, please."

"And I'll have Scotch," commanded Pete, loudly from his chair.

"It's not Sunday, dear," said Polly to Pete. To me, she added, sotto voce, "He only has Scotch on Sundays."

"Damn Sunday!" Pete exclaimed. "We have a guest. It's a special night. Give me Scotch. One for the road." His blue eyes glared ferociously.

"All right, dear," said Polly, long-sufferingly. "Shall it be our Scotch or Jeremy's?"

Their Scotch was a minor brand and there wasn't much left in the bottle; mine was Chivas Regal.

"Oh his, *his*," cried Pete, impatiently adding, "if he doesn't mind, that is."

Halfway through his glass of Chivas Regal, Pete put aside the *Japan Times* and looked at me. I was back on the sofa with my whisky. "I never finished my story about Jeremy Cottrell in Baghdad," he said. "One morning around lunch time, I was driving down Rashid Street and by chance Cottrell was in front of me in an Iraqi army jeep. We were stuck in a traffic jam—Rashid Street was often bunged up. Suddenly Cottrell—he was a major then—jumped out of his jeep and started to beat the car in front with his swagger cane shouting, "Get on, you idiot!" or something like that. He was in uniform. Irascible chap he was. Never married as far as I know." Pete sipped his whisky. I sipped mine.

"And then?" I asked.

Pete frowned. "And then, what?"

What happened then?"

"Nothing. He got back into his jeep and eventually the traffic moved on."

"I see."

"Extraordinary chap, Cottrell."

"Ready!" cried Polly from the bar.

I looked round. She had dished up the food. There were steaming plates of something on the counter. Pete rose and he and I climbed on to barstools. Polly perched opposite us on the other side. "Ah, cottage pie!" said Pete. "Good old cottage pie! Better than some Jap stuff, isn't it? What about some wine, Polly?"

"It isn't Sunday, Pete."

"You said that before. It's guest night, though. Open a bottle."

"Which one, dear?" Polly asked, timidly.

Was she afraid of him now that he had had two gins and tonic and three whiskies and soda? Did he beat her? The angry glare that had come into his eyes suggested that he was capable of it.

"What about that one?" he said, pointing to the shelf. "The one lying next the bottle of Grand Marnier."

"We were going to save that for Christmas."

"Never mind about Christmas. Let's have it now. I may be dead by Christmas."

Polly took the recumbent bottle from the shelf with a shrug which said "Have it your own way!" and went into the kitchen. When she brought the bottle back, opened, she said, "Oughtn't we to let it breathe?"

"No. Pour it out. Lot of nonsense all this letting wine breathe, don't you think, Jeremy?"

"Well, I'm not so sure about that. It depends on the age of the wine, I think."

"In a restaurant one drinks wine just opened, doesn't one?"

Polly took three glasses which had been lying upside-down on the shelf and poured out the wine.

"Yes," I agreed. "But haven't you found that the second glass tastes better than the first?"

"Don't know about that. Well, here's luck!"

We raised our glasses and then tasted the wine. It was an excellent claret.

After the pie came fresh peaches, over which Polly poured some of the wine, rather to the disgust of the colonel. "A waste," he said. "No, it isn't," she dared reply, "peaches and wine are so much nicer than peaches and cream. Don't you think so, Jeremy?"

Embarrassed to take sides, I said, weakly, "I like both. The peaches are very good here."

Polly took our plates into the kitchen and came back with a little round box of Camembert.

"You have been extravagant," reprimanded Pete. "Cheese is so expensive here, you know."

"Cheese seems to be expensive everywhere these days," I said. Polly extricated the cheese from its box and its wrapping and put it on a plate. I cut a thin slice for myself.

"This frozen Camembert isn't much good," grumbled Pete. He was right, but I didn't like to say so. I had no desire to appear to favor one spouse over the other. "It's only the hard cheese that can stand being frozen," continued Pete. "You should have got Gruyère while you were in your reckless mood, not this flavorless soap." Nevertheless, the colonel ate his generous helping and cut himself another slice.

Pete and I resumed our previous places by the television set. He took up the *Japan Times*, in which he seemed to find much more to read than I had ever done. I looked at the portrait of the stripling officer whose Sam Browne gave him a wasp waist. The years had ravaged the face more than the figure; the innocence and the expectation in the bright blue eyes had faded into a defeated-yet-defiant look; the corners of the mouth, turning up hopefully in the painting, now drooped; the bare upper lip of the youthful officer was now covered by a white colonel's moustache; the brown hair and the eyebrows had become snowy; the nose had broadened at the base; the forehead was lined; there were crow's feet; the shoulders were slightly rounded, but being spare he had no paunch to speak of. He was still, it seemed, in fine fettle; good for many years. How old was he? Over seventy since he was commissioned before the second world war. I again regarded the portrait.

"That's when I'd just got my commission," said Pete. "My mother insisted on my being painted. There's still a likeness, don't you think?"

"Oh yes, indeed. What a waist you had!"

"The artist exaggerated a bit." Pete let out a grunt of a laugh. "Polly thinks I oughtn't to have the thing so prominently displayed, but it's by a respectable artist, and we've hung it in all our various homes." He glanced at the traveling clock. "By Jove, it's news time!

Do you mind pushing the bottom button on the old box?"

I did so and the nine o'clock news began. The items were mostly about domestic incidents and, of course, all of them were reported in Japanese. Polly arrived from the kitchen and sat in *her* chair opposite her husband, from whom came quiet snores; the *Japan Times* had slipped out of his hands on to the floor. I watched the pictures on the screen trying to guess what they concerned. Polly took out of a capacious cloth bag by her chair a piece of gros point and began to stitch; now and then she gave the screen a glance.

"I suppose you can understand it all," I said to her.

"Only little bits. I can understand the weather at the end." She gave a shy little laugh. "There are signs; little umbrellas for rain, tiny clouds when it's to be overcast, and little suns when it's to be sunny. Rather sweet."

I rose. "I'm a bit tired. I think I'd like to go to bed. What time is breakfast?"

"Eight. We have to go to the bathroom in turns. Like most bathrooms in Japanese houses it's on the ground floor, or the first floor as they call it. He," she poked her needle in the direction of Pete, "has his shower at seven-thirty, so you can have yours either at about ten to eight or before at seven or seven-fifteen. I have mine at six-thirty. What do you like for breakfast? We just have continental. No eggs."

"That'll do fine."

"Cornflakes?"

"No thanks. Just coffee and toast, and perhaps some fruit."

"Good. I'll say good night, then."

"Goodnight, Polly."

I read until after midnight when Polly and Pete came up the stairs to their bedroom. Pete's mutterings were punctuated by Polly's shushes.

"He's not asleep. His light's still on." I heard Pete say.

"Perhaps he's fallen asleep with it on."

"I hope not."

"Shush!"

I chose the later hour which Polly had suggested for my ablutions, and as a result did not arrive at the breakfast table—the meal was taken in the kitchen—till ten past eight. Pete was sitting at the head of the table with a little transistor set clapped to his ear.

"Shush," said Polly with a finger to her mouth. "The BBC news."

I could only hear a distorted voice and atmospherics. Polly pointed at various breakfast ingredients. The colonel's dull eyes caught mine. He nodded and indicated the radio at his ear with his other hand. I helped myself to coffee and toast.

"Any news?" asked Polly when Pete had at last silenced the crackling and put the radio on the table.

"None. Nothing of interest, anyway." He took a piece of toast, spread it with butter and spooned on to his plate a good dollop of marmalade. "Tried any of this stuff?" he asked, pushing the jar towards me. "Polly makes it. It's top-hole, better than the Japanese muck. They don't know how to make proper marmalade. Much too sweet. Polly puts lemons with the oranges, don't you, Poll?"

"And grapefruit."

"I've just taken some," I said. "It is good."

"Now," Pete continued, "about this morning. Got any plans? I go to my den after breakfast to work. Later, around noon, we go to the beach and have a swim and a picnic lunch. Does that suit you?"

"Sounds fine."

"What's on your program, Polly?" Pete's morning manner was that of the grumpy colonel in the mess after a guest night. I wondered if he were putting on this authoritative air for my benefit, or if when alone with his wife he addressed her as he would his adjutant.

"I'm going shopping. Perhaps, Jeremy, you'd like to come with me. You'll see a bit of the countryside."

The marks between the colonel's eyebrows furrowed. "But you went shopping yesterday."

"I forgot some things, darling." I noticed the wink she gave her husband but he didn't seem to. He said, "Daily visits into town are very wasteful. You ought to learn to shop for the week. Well, sitting here won't get any work done." He rose. She winked at him again and this time he registered the signal by closing his eyes and nodding slightly.

"What is Pete's work?" I asked Polly when we had driven a few hundred yards from the house.

"He's writing a book."

"What about?"

"Japan, I think. He never discusses it, never lets me see it."

"How odd."

"He is rather odd, as I expect you've noticed." She turned into a main road joining a line of traffic. "When we first came here there were hardly any cars."

"Do you have any friends here?"

"Not really, unless one calls Mr. Maeda a friend."

"Who's he?"

"He used to be a student of Pete's. Pete gave him conversation lessons. Now he teaches English at a school in the district. He sometimes visits us."

In spite of the cars and the trucks the road was pretty with rich green rice fields and trees on either side of it and beyond steep hills thickly wooded with dark green Japanese cypresses. In contrast, the town was an ugly little place of concrete blocks tempered by a few narrow streets of wooden houses with shops forming their ground floors. We called first at a supermarket where Polly filled her basket with fruit and vegetables, three steaks on plastic plates sealed with polythene and some Ementhal and Australian cheddah cheese. Each time she picked up a bunch of turnips, the steaks, a small musk melon she asked for my approval. "Can you eat this?" she asked. Like her husband I wondered why she hadn't done all this shopping yesterday until at the pay-out counter she fumbled in her handbag and said, "Damn! I've forgotten my purse." I paid or she did with the ten thousand yen note I gave her. I guessed that Pete kept her short of housekeeping money. In a drink shop she took up a bottle of gin. "Do you like Gordons or Beefeaters?" she asked. And then, "Smirnoff or Polish vodka?" She did the same with some bottles of wine. "French or Spanish?" I had to give her another ten thousand yen note. We set off for home. "How terrible of me to have forgotten my purse," she said, laughing. "What can you be thinking?" I didn't tell her that because of those winks

I was wondering whether she had forgotten her purse on purpose. Instead, I asked, "Don't you ever feel lonely, cut off?"

"Pete and I are very self-contained, you know."

When we arrived at the house I helped Polly unload the car and carry her or rather my purchases into the kitchen. Pete was ensconced in his den.

Polly began to make ham and egg sandwiches for our picnic. I hovered about uselessly for a while and then went upstairs to fetch the book I was reading, descended and sat on the sofa. I longed for Monday to come. I couldn't help thinking about the twenty thousand yen I'd lent Polly; after all, it was about eighty pounds. And she hadn't spent it all. She might have given me the change. It was pleasant reading in the comfortable room. I was enjoying Bruce Chatwin's essays and now and then allowed my eyes to wander away from the page and regard the trunks and branches of the pines outside the window and the creek below, when Pete came in from his den, which led directly into the sitting room. He locked the door and put the key in the pocket of his khaki shorts before advancing into the room. He gave a start when he caught me looking at him. "Oh!" Didn't see you. I've done my morning stint. You can't be too careful. You ready for the beach?"

"Yes, I suppose so. I haven't any beach clothes."

"Just come as you are. Polly! Ready?"

We set off in the car, parked it in the station yard and walked down through a charming narrow street of open, windowless shops to the water's edge, where, from a landing stage, a ferry boat took us and a handful of Japanese across the bay to the bar of land that protected it from the ocean. There were attractive views of the forested hills and of the lagoon. It was a sunny day, the sky decorated with fine weather clouds. We disembarked and walked—the colonel leading, Polly behind him with the picnic basket and me bringing up the rear with the traveling rug Polly had asked me to carry—along a winding path between bungalows almost hidden by walls of sand to a beach where there were cafes and bathing establishments. A sunburnt lad in swimming briefs, a T-shirt and a basket hat came running up.

"Hello, Tanaka-san. *Genki deska? Konnichi wa*," said Pete.

"*Konnichi wa*, Johnson-san." The lad beamed and followed

us to the beach of gray volcanic sand; he carried an umbrella and a deck chair which he had fetched from one of the bathing establishments. He planted the umbrella, set up the chair, took the rug from me and spread it on the ground. Pete sat in the chair and Polly on the rug. I stood wondering what to do. The lad trotted off. "We've only one chair," Polly apologized. "The boy looks after it and the umbrella for us."

"I think I'll have a swim." I went back to the nearest bathing establishment and changed, putting my clothes into a plastic basket which I checked in with the woman in charge. By the time I got back to my host and hostess, Pete was in swimming shorts and Polly in a bathing costume that was stretched to its limits by her bulging flesh. Pete's chest was a mat of white hair. We went down to the water, which was as calm as the lagoon. Pete did a belly flop and swam out to sea, Polly in a white bathing cap that accentuated her ruddy face bobbed about in the shallows, and I did my favorite side stroke bringing my left arm out of the water. I remained within shouting distance of Polly. "Does Pete always swim so far out?"

"He's a strong swimmer. I must say, though, I'm relieved when he turns back. There are all sorts of currents." She looked out to sea. Pete's white head was a dark dot.

Pete returned at last and we went up the beach to the little piece of black sticky sand the Crosby-Johnsons had staked out for themselves. Polly and Pete wrapped towels round their bodies and sat down: he in the chair, she on the rug. I hesitated, and then went off to the bathing establishment to change—I hate sitting about in wet swim shorts. When I returned, Pete had a drink in his hand and Polly, who had changed back into her cotton dress, was unpacking the picnic basket. "I've brought a beer for you," she said.

Pete said, "It doesn't taste like Japanese gin, Polly."

"It's Gordons."

"You extravagant girl!"

"Jeremy bought it for us," said Polly, not looking at me.

"Good of you, old boy. If you knew how I loathed Japanese gin! It's all we can afford." He took a sip from his glass, sighed and mumbled, "Good to be here, eh? Better than Blighty, what? Thank

God we're not there, eh Polly? August in England: no sun, dark skies, rain."

Looking at the uninviting beach, I remarked, "Last summer was glorious in England. Day after day of sunshine."

"You have that once in ten years," countered Pete.

"Do you ever go to England?" I asked.

Pete replied, "No, thank Heavens! It's a foreign land to us, isn't it, Polly?"

Polly didn't reply. She busied herself with the picnic basket, opening a plastic box containing sandwiches. "Jeremy also bought us some wine," she announced, wanting, I suspected, to change a sore subject.

"By Jove, how splendid!"

Thinking of the twenty thousand yen, I calculated that the amount wouldn't have been enough for two nights in the nearby tourist hotel and that was some compensation. I soon finished my small bottle of beer, and when the sandwiches had been consumed and Pete had emptied his thermos flask of gin and tonic (I was offered none), he pushed the round white hat he was wearing over his eyes and leaned back in his chair. Polly stretched out on the rug, her head on a rolled up towel. There was no room for me so I went to one of the cafés and had another beer and some noodles.

We got back to the house at five. Polly went into the kitchen, Pete to his den. I lay on my bed wondering if I could somehow send myself an urgent message calling me back to Tokyo.

The routine was no different from that of the previous evening, except that I refused to have beer foisted on me and insisted on Scotch. Pete didn't say anything but his expression revealed his disapproval of my helping to deplete the bottle I had brought. We perched again at the bar facing Polly, who had done the steaks à point. She was a good cook. We had one of the bottles of *my* wine.

"Where's this wine come from?" asked Pete.

"Bourgogne."

"Where?"

"Burgundy."

"Jeremy bought it for us." Polly avoided my look. I then

guessed that I would not be getting my money back. It was very bourgeois of me to think of the eighty pounds, but understandable, surely.

After the meal Pete sat in his chair and I on the sofa. Just before news time, Pete said, "Tomorrow's Sunday. We have church."

"Church? Is there a church here?"

"There is one, but not of the right kind. Anyway, the services are in Japanese. We have our church here. I hope you'll join us. We have it after breakfast."

"I should be pleased to." I was curious to know what the service consisted of. Would the colonel don clerical garb?

I went down to breakfast the next morning a little later than on the previous day. The transistor radio was by Pete's plate, switched off. Pete was wearing a dark blue suit, Polly a blue dress with long sleeves. It was too hot for such Sunday clothes and I challenged the look of disapproval my open-necked shirt and slacks received by saying, "It's a bit warm to dress up, isn't it? I thought you said the *service* was to be in the house. Sort of family prayers, is it?"

"Not exactly," answered Pete, his pale blue eyes flicking away from mine.

"We like to feel we're in church," Polly explained.

"But if you—" I stopped myself.

"If we what?" demanded Pete.

"Never mind."

"No. Tell us what you were going to say, please," insisted the colonel. "If we, what?"

Embarrassed, I said, "I was going to say that if you dislike England so much and never want to go back there, why do you wish to observe such a British institution as church on Sunday?"

"Matter of discipline and tradition. Surely, that's obvious." He looked at his watch. "Church in twenty minutes, then. By the way, Polly, I thought we'd take Cottrell to Ise this afternoon. He ought to see the shrine. We could have another picnic." He looked at me and added, "We don't go to the beach on

Sundays."

I nearly asked if this was because it was Sunday or because of the crowds. I went upstairs during the interval between breakfast and *church*, and when I descended to the sitting room I saw that the sofa had been pushed back and three upright chairs had been placed in front of it. On top of the television set was a tape recorder. The air-cooler was on and the temperature in the room was pleasant. Pete was standing by the window looking at the gnarled and twisted trunks of the pines and the water below. Polly entered with two copies of the BBC hymn book. "Shall we begin?"

"All right," answered Pete advancing from the window.

Polly sat in the middle chair and signed to me to take the chair on her left. "Which is it today?" she asked her husband.

"I've chosen one of the services from St. Martin's in the Fields."

"Good. They're always nice."

Pete turned on the tape recorder and Matins from the famous church crackled forth. The first hymn was "The Church's one foundation, is Jesus Christ her Lord, She is His new creation, By water and the Word..." And Pete, on his wife's right, as if at the aisle side of the pew, began to sing the peculiar words in a baritone voice that he obviously thought better than it was. Polly held the hymnal so that I could see it, but my singing consisted of trying to suppress giggles. We knelt when the invisible congregation knelt, stood when they did, and sat during the sermon. We knelt again for the blessing and stood for the final hymn, at the end of which Pete turned off the machine. He took on that self-congratulatory, smug air that some people adopt after coming out of church, as if they have done something worthy and should be commended. I could imagine him and Polly outside a parish church in a Sussex village talking to fellow members of the congregation. Polly said, "It's a pity not to have the service live, but England is eight hours behind, so we can't. Pete has recorded a number of BBC services. Isn't it a good idea?"

"Yes," I answered uncertainly.

Pete removed the tape and showed it to me. "I have them all marked, you see." He carried the machine and the tape into his den, while I helped Polly put the sofa and the chairs back into their usual places.

Pete emerged. "No work today, of course. So let's go and change." He looked at me. "You're already changed, of course. We'll move off in half an hour, right?" He started to mount the stairs, stopped, turned and cried out to Polly, who had gone to the kitchen, "Polly, don't forget to turn off the air cooler!" He continued his ascent.

Two lines of cars choked the road to Ise.

"*Nichio drivar*. Sunday drivers," said the colonel.

"That's what the Japanese call those who only drive their cars on Sundays." The cars edged along: one line going towards Kashikojima, the other to Toba and the holy Shinto shrine. Our approach to the shrine, after we had managed to park the car, up a wide avenue of majestic Japanese cedars and through two arches was shared with hundreds of trippers. The shrine complex nestles among the huge cedars. In an inner courtyard is the Main Hall, which may only be entered by Imperial personages or envoys. The site is ancient but the buildings are demolished every twenty years and rebuilt.

We stood outside the thatched gateway to the Main Hall together with a battalion of tourists. "It was to this spot," murmured Pete into my ear, "that the Sun Goddess Amaterasu sent down her son, Jimmu, from heaven to become the first emperor." He spoke as if he believed the myth. "In the shrine sanctum are kept the three sacred treasures: the Mirror, the Sword and the Jewel. The Japanese gods didn't have bodies. They resided in things known as *shintai* or god bodies. Amaterasu's god body is a mirror. Members of the Imperial family come here to commune with their ancestors. The new Emperor Akihito will come here and commune with the Sun Goddess. He becomes the Sun Goddess, and then takes the human form again, or something like that."

"He becomes a mirror?" I asked.

"He is sort of absorbed into heaven or into a heavenly body, a god body, I suppose. Something like that, anyway," replied Pete, explaining or rather not explaining in a vague Japanese fashion.

We went on to Toba, visited the Mikimoto pearl islet, where we inspected the process of pearl culture and watched some girls in white diving suits submerge and bring up from the depths seaweed instead of oysters. We took a boat to a little island, where we sat on a crowded beach and picnicked on ham, egg and tomato sandwiches.

"We ought to have brought our bathing costumes," said Pete, sipping his gin and tonic.

"Why on earth didn't we?" asked Polly from under her broad-brimmed straw hat.

"It didn't occur to me that we might come here."

"Nor to me either. How silly of us! I'd love a dip." Polly laughed her laugh that sounded forced rather than natural and jolly. She seemed, though, an even tempered woman, which was just as well as she had to put up with Pete.

Drinking my beer, I felt resentful, like a boy not considered old enough to have spirits. The beach was covered with gray stones and the sand between them was gray, and black when moistened by the surge of a broken wave. Children ran about screaming. I wished I could pass out until the next day when I was going back to Tokyo. Even my confined quarters seemed attractive at this moment.

We returned at a snail's pace to Kashikojima. When we got into the house, I felt I ought to behave like a good guest and invite my host and hostess to dinner at the tourist hotel. I did so. Polly said, "But you've done so much for us already." I gathered from this statement that I would definitely not be getting my twenty-thousand yen back.

Drinks and dinner at the monstrously expensive tourist hotel set me back more than another twenty-thousand yen; fortunately I was able to use my credit card. We had the table d'hôte menu: corn soup (rather a favorite in Japanese Western restaurants; probably introduced by the Americans), steak, salad, ice cream and a bottle of claret. We all plumped for steak, although we had had it the night before, because it was beef from nearby Matsuzaka, the most delectable beef in Japan and the most costly; the cows are said to be given beer and massage. During the meal, Pete (he had had three glasses of whisky) got on to his old friend Cottrell again. "Ten years ago. Was it ten, Polly?"

"More than that, dear. We've been here fifteen."

"Isn't it frightful how time flies! It was just before we came here. Must have been seventeen years ago, 1973. We thought we'd try Cyprus. Didn't like it. Yearned to return to Japan. The Far East gets you. Anyway, we ran into old Cottrell in the harbor in Kyrenia, where we were staying. He was completely bedraggled, in rags, almost. He had sailed round the Panhandle from Famagusta, got caught in a squall, boat capsized, managed to swim ashore. Lost everythIng: passport, travelers' checks, every damned thing. Since his retirement he'd been living in a boat, all by himself. He seemed a bit crazed; mind you, he was always a bit odd, but a first class instructor. I'll say that for him. We put him up in our rented house till his money came through from London. Never heard from him again. No bread and butter letter even. I wonder what's happened to him."

I made a mental note to be sure to write Polly a thank-you note. I wondered if Cottrell ever wondered what happened to Polly and Pete. I felt I'd like to meet him to tell him.

In the trains back to Tokyo I kept looking up from my book and gazing unseeingly out of the window and thinking about Polly and Pete. My thoughts almost obliterated the swiftly passing scene, which, anyway, was houses, factories, factories, houses most of the way. What was Pete writing? What had he meant when he said "You can't be too careful" after locking the door of his den? Did he lock it against Polly rather than thieves? In Japan burglary isn't nearly so common as it is in the rest of the world, and in Kagoshima it was probably very rare. How lonely were the retired colonel and his lady? How hard up were they? Did they really "love it here"? Was Kashikojima, where they seemed to speak to no one but shop assistants and waiters, really better than Crowborough, Bournemouth or Torquay? I laughed out loud startling my Japanese neighbor on the bullet train when I recalled the Sunday *service.* How could Polly take it seriously? I imagined Pete becoming more peculiar and donning a cassock and surplice and giving the blessing to his congregation of one. While some people imagine themselves as orchestra conductors, others think of themselves as priests. I laughed at the thought of Pete preaching to Polly. My neighbor, a man in his fifties, gave me a wary look. Most Japanese think that foreigners are an odd breed.

Three months later my negotiations were nearly complete. I had made a business trip to England in the meantime. My sister, who lives in Horsham, came up to London and we lunched at my club. She enjoyed my account of the visit to Polly and Pete. Of course I exaggerated their oddity and we laughed a lot. The friends who had told her about them and requested me to look them up were no more than dinner-party acquaintances, who probably, when my sister mentioned that she had a brother in Japan, wanted to cap her statement and boast about their friends in that country.

I returned to my "rabbit hutch" (the Japanese resented the European Community's official's remark about their being workaholics living in rabbit hutches) to wind up agreements, sign contracts and so on. I had about a month to go when one Saturday morning in November (I gave myself a five-day week) while I was contemplating getting out of bed, the telephone rang. It was Polly.

"May I come round to see you?"

"Now?"

"Yes. I'm at the station."

"Which station?"

"Your station. It's such a maze I can't find the way. Could you come and meet me?"

"This apartment block is easy to find." I gave her directions and asked her not to come round for half an hour. I rose, washed and dressed hurriedly, cursing as I did so.

Polly wore a shabby brown tweed coat over the dark blue Sunday dress she had put on for the service. The kerchief round her head made her resemble a refugee. She placed her grip on my tiny entrance step and after I had helped her off with her coat, I ushered her into my dollhouse room. She held on to an ominously bulging shopping bag. Publishers can smell out a manuscript. I had not had time to fold up the bed, which turned into a seat as hard as one on a subway train. The only other seats in the room were a canvas director's chair and a folding chair made for a very small bottom. I sat Polly in the former and put myself on the latter, which was by the desk-cum-dining table. There were only a few feet between us. The proximity was embarrassing.

"What may I offer you? Coffee?"

"Pete's dead."

"I am sorry. I am very sorry."

"He had a fatal heart attack at his desk in his den. I found him there at lunchtime."

"He looked quite well last summer."

"He wasn't really. Angina. He took pills."

"When did it happen?"

"A week ago. We had a Buddist funeral. Our old friend, Maeda, who used to be Pete's pupil, helped enormously. One of the ideas of our going to Kashikojima was for Pete to give English lessons. Maeda was the only student he got. He proved a loyal friend and arranged everything. He took it all out of my hands. The funeral was awful." She spoke quickly as if it was a relief to unburden herself of the tale; I was probably the only other person she had related her experience to. "First," she went on, "Pete was put in an open coffin in the house behind a bank of flowers—all done by Maeda and the undertaker. Some people from the hotel came to attend the wake: the barmen and three of the waiters, good of them. A Buddhist priest recited the sutras or something. It's a wonder Pete didn't turn in his coffin. Do you know what Maeda suggested?"

"No."

"He suggested that since Pete liked swimming his swimming shorts should be put in the coffin; apparently the Japanese put something the dead person was fond of in the coffin. Of course I didn't agree to anything so silly." Polly attempted a laugh which turned into a sob. Tears ran down her cheeks. She mopped them with a screwed-up handkerchief. "Then the next day we went to the crematorium. You've never been to a Japanese funeral, I suppose."

"No."

"Then don't go. Do you know what they do?"

I shook my head.

"One looks at the face through a little window in the coffin. Maeda said, 'Take a last look.' Poor Pete. He looked so very dead. Then while the body is being burned, the mourners—in this case only Maeda and me—go into a sort of waiting room. Beer was served. I drank a whole bottle, a large one." Another laugh was defeated by a sob. "And then we were summoned into a hall which contained tables bearing trays of bones. Several funerals were going on at the same time. I don't know how they know which bones are whose. Do you know what we were supposed to do?"

"No, what?"

"With long iron chopsticks pick up the bones and drop them into an urn. They were recognizable—the bones, I mean. I don't know how they do it. Anyway, I just couldn't do it, not that I'm clumsy with chopsticks." Polly gave a wan smile. "I just couldn't do it. It was so macabre. I ran out of the building and waited for Maeda, who appeared eventually with the urn. Do you know what he said? He said it was lucky to chopstick the collar bone into the urn and he, my not being there, had chopsticked both. Can you imagine? He seemed quite bucked about it. Aren't *they* peculiar?"

"What have you done with the urn?"

"It's in the house at Kashikojima, in Pete's den. I can't bear its being there. It's so hard to find a burial plot here. People reserve them almost at birth."

"What will you do?"

"Take it back to England, I suppose."

"You won't stay on in Japan?"

"Can't possibly afford to, and besides, I hate it here."

"Oh?"

"Yes. I pretended I loved it for Pete's sake."

"You'll sell the house?"

"Yes, of course."

"It ought to be worth a lot. Property being so high in Japan."

"I hope to sell it to a Nagoya millionaire who wants a *besso*, a second house. I don't know how I'll manage. Pete's pension will be halved. Pete was selling capital to make ends meet. I don't know how much is left. Precious little, I expect. I'll have my old age pension, but that won't go far. Pete never really thought of me." She burst into tears.

I looked at the aging woman. Her face red, her gray hair straggled, she seemed about to break down. Our inevitable proximity in the minuscule room made the situation comic. I wanted to laugh. What was I to do with this distraught woman? Why had she come to see me? I soon got the answer to the second question. My guess had been correct She pulled out of her shopping bag a brown paper parcel.

"Pete's book?" I queried.

"Yes"

"What's it about?"

"It's supposed to be a book about Japan. It begins that way, but turns into an attack, a diatribe against me."

"Against you?"

"Yes. Have you a bathroom?"

I stood up to allow her to squeeze past me and make her way, sideways by my bed, to the "cupboard" bathroom, a one piece unit all made of plastic. I handed her a towel through the door. "Exiguous," she said.

When she reappeared she seemed to have recovered from her woebegone, pitiful state. She had applied a little make-up and tidied her hair and presumably washed her face. She was like the Polly I had met at Kashikojima, but no longer dependent; she suddenly seemed self-reliant, businesslike. I was astonished that twenty minutes in my midget bathroom could make such a difference. I think she had sensed my lack of concern for her plight and realized the need to be sensible and practical and that playing the "pity-me" card wouldn't work.

"I feel better," she said.

She squeezed past me again and sat in the director's chair. I resumed my place at the desk.

"What was I saying?" she asked.

"You said that the book began about Japan and then—"

"Yes, yes. As I said it turned into a diatribe against me, which reveals that Pete really loathed me, and Japan."

"But why did you—"

"Stay on? Stay together? We had nowhere else to go. Burnt our boats. I had nowhere else to go. We have no children to sponge off, no relations at all. I just had to stick it out. Also, I was afraid of him."

"Afraid?"

"Yes. It's hard to express. I was afraid of his tongue. It could be so sharp and hurtful. I was afraid of being belittled, made to look a fool, to feel a fool. Fear plays a big part in relationships, you know, or perhaps you don't know. Much more than people realize. People, those who are afraid, don't like to admit it, even to themselves. I abated his wrath by giving in to him, to his merest whim."

"And was one of his whims holding that Sunday *service?*"

"Yes, indeed it was. The first time we had a service I laughed and he turned his fury on to me. I had to go along with it. Being such an arch egoist, he was blind to anyone else's feelings. He assumed that my sacrifices were his due. He never considered for a moment that I might want a change sometimes." Polly sat up straight. "Now, I'm not such an ass as to think that his writing on Japan is of any value at all, but what I think might be is the story this book—she put a hand on the parcel on the desk—contains. I mean the story of two people, hating each other and their surroundings, but putting up with their circumstances simply because they had no choice to do otherwise. It is the story of a living hell."

"Many marriages are that."

"Of course. I think, though, that this story is rather special. Not because it is about me. I want you to read it and consider it for publication."

"I'll certainly read it. I can't make any promises, though. How can I get in touch with you?"

"I'll be at Kashikojima for the next two months, at least." She rose. "I must be going."

"Can't I give you lunch? There's a Western-style hotel nearby that has an excellent coffee shop."

"No thanks. I'm going straight back to Kashikojima. I came up to Tokyo on Thursday. Saw the British Consul and the bank yesterday. I must get back today. Tokyo is fiendishly expensive, for me, anyway. I stayed in what they call a business hotel. I had a tiny room, like this one, and it cost the earth." At the door, she said, "I haven't forgotten the twenty-thousand yen I borrowed from you. Pete put me up to it. He wanted gin and we were short. I wanted the steaks. The first we'd had for ages. And you gave us steak, much better steak, at the hotel. You can deduct the amount from the advance for the book." She laughed and was gone.

I would have liked to have seen the expression on her face after her departure. Did it lapse into one of sorrow and resignation? It seemed that the bathroom had been a dressing room in which she had stepped into another role. If she had hated her husband so much, why should she grieve? I supposed she was really grieving for herself and her predicament. Why though had she lied to me and said it was Pete who had put her up to pretending she had forgotten her purse on that shopping morning? Surely it was her ruse since she had winked at her husband when he had complained about her going to the shops two days running?

I took the manuscript to the coffee shop of the Western-style hotel which I often patronized at the weekend. The headwaiter greeted me cordially and conducted me to my favorite table at banquette one in a corner. I ordered lamb chops and a glass of the white house-wine and opened the manuscript at random.

The book began fifteen years before when the Crosby-Johnsons returned to Japan from Cyprus. It was a muddle of a book, full of rambling about Pete's views on Japan and the Japanese. Interlarded between the descriptions were criticisms of Polly. Many of them bitter.

The first part was a jeremiad against certain old colleagues in the Embassy and officials in the Japanese Foreign Office and the Self-Defense Department, who didn't have much time for the Crosby-Johnsons now that the colonel was retired "They were polite but cold" Pete wrote. "I am experiencing what many retired people have to face: a demotion, a degradation...Tokyo is too expensive. I've decided to go to Kashikojima, which Polly and I liked when we spent a weekend there during my time at the Embassy...

"I've found a plot of land on a hill with a view of Ago Bay and among pines. Polly, typically, was no help at all. She dithered."

I turned over some pages. After a guide-bookish account of the shrine at Ise, the Sun Goddess Amaterasu and her son, Jimmu, there followed a description of the building of the house, which Pete was supervising: "A terrible day today. Polly interfered or tried to over the layout downstairs. She wants the counter of the bar in the sitting room to have a flap so one can enter the room from the bar. Quite unnecessary and more expensive. Polly can come round from the kitchen and I can sit on the sitting room side of the bar for meals and she can be on the bar side facing me There will, of course, be access to the bar from the kitchen. I got my way."

Polly had penciled in the margin: "He never admitted how awkward it was not being able to go from the kitchen through the bar into the sitting room. Going round by the hall was a trek. And I had to do this when he wanted his evening whisky."

Further on I read: "Our furniture has arrived from England, where it has been in store. A great row with Polly over my portrait. She wanted it in the hall. I insisted that it must be put above the fireplace. I had my way." Scribbled in the margin by Polly was: "One of the few times I stood up to Pete. I did not want his silly portrait dominating the room. Having him in the flesh was more than enough. I gave in for the sake of peace, but not before we had screamed abuse at each other."

After an intelligent and detailed description of the cultivation of oysters, came, "Polly complained about the frosted glass in the bedroom windows today. She wanted ordinary glass. I told her that it was too late and anyway it was the custom in Japan to have what they call *kumori* (cloudy) glass in bedrooms so that neighbours can't look in. I refused to have the glass changed." Polly had written: "I pointed out that the best view was from the bedroom and there weren't any neighbors. Pete said there would be neighbors in the future. He was probably right about this. I did say that there were such things as curtains. He won, of course, and so we had to put up with that beastly lavatory glass in the bedroom."

Pete wrote: "When I write these impressions of Japan and the Japanese, which, I think, are of interest, I find my mind invaded by Polly and her irritating habits. She is so forgetful. She goes into the little town for shopping and always forgets something essential, so she has to go shopping again the following day. Yesterday, she forgot to buy some sugar so back she has to go this morning. Such a waste. Petrol is very dear here. What isn't!" Polly wrote: "I usually forgot something on purpose so I could make another trip into town. Any excuse to escape for a while. Later, there was a proper reason."

"The Japanese," Pete wrote, "suffer from a pathological shyness. I find this maddening. In conversation the ball is always in my court. When I have thought of something to say, I immediately have to think of what I shall say after the subject is exhausted. They never contribute anything at all. If one says nothing, they say nothing. It's due to their dearth of English, I suppose. They chatter enough among themselves, and yet are tongue-tied when with a foreigner."

Polly's remark about this observation read: "It's Pete's attitude that is wrong. He glares at them (the Japanese) as if they were raw recruits. I told him that if approached with a smile he'd get a different reaction. I know the Japanese feel afraid when a big-nosed foreigner glowers at them with his huge eyes. They dislike eye contact, and they find blue eyes very strange. They wonder if a blue-eyed person can see properly. Also they are not embarrassed by silence as Westerners are."

About his pupil Pete wrote: "Maeda is a dull stick and can't get anything right. He will say 'I lead' when he means 'I read' in spite of my making him repeat the words over and over again. And he has no idea of tenses at all. 'Yesterday I go,' he says. 'You went,' I correct. 'You went,' he repeats. 'No, not you went, I went. Where did you go yesterday?' 'Yesterday, I go...' So it continues. We get nowhere. Polly says he's a nice chap. He may be, but he's a frightful pupil. And he teaches English! God help the Japanese! No wonder they speak English so frightfully, though they seem to have done all right without knowing the language. Polly is no judge of people at all. She has not the least understanding of the Japanese."

Polly put, "Maeda was a sweet man. He was nervous and Pete made him more so. He spoke quite good English when he was alone with me. He would come into the kitchen after his lesson and we'd chat. 'I wish you would teach me,' he once said."

Further on there was more about Maeda. "I'm not sure that Maeda isn't getting a little too fond of Polly" came after an account of visiting a potter near the town of Tsu, not far from Kashikojima. The colonel seemed to have a taste for ceramics and described competently the making of pots. Maeda accompanied them to the pottery. "I caught Polly and Maeda spooning behind the car after I had been watching the potter throw his clay. I didn't say anything but Maeda understood my look of displeasure and didn't come for his lesson for three weeks."

Polly wrote: "We weren't spooning as Pete puts it in his old-fashioned way. Not then, anyway. We were just talking, neither of us being interested in watching the potter work. I don't think at that time Maeda thought of me in sexual terms. I did find him handsome, though. He had such nice hair, raven black, and a charming straight nose, down which I longed to run my finger, and his ebony eyes glinted like polished onyx. He was thirty and not yet married. I think he found me motherly and kept up the lessons with Pete so that he could talk to me afterwards. He's now married. Pete and I had a terrible row when we got home after the visit to the pottery. A real shouting match which ended in his having chest pains, gasping for breath, and shaking. 'You did this,' he accused when he was feeling better. We didn't speak for several days. We did go and see a doctor in Nagoya who diagnosed angina and prescribed pills. Pete was told he'd be all right if he took them regularly."

There followed about fifty pages on the insularity of the Jepanese, the closing of Japan during the Tokugawa period being the principal cause. I skipped these pages until I came across: "I'm not going to challenge Polly again but I didn't hear Maeda's car start up and drive off from the house until about forty minutes after he'd left my den when the lesson was over. He comes at nine-thirty for an hour, then leaves me to get on with my writing. Polly then gives him coffee in the kitchen and off he goes. But yesterday morning he stayed longer than usual, much longer. I have my suspicions. With his limited powers of conversation in English they can't be talking all the time, or can they? The conversation hour I have with him seems like five hours and· much of the time is spent in silence. I haven't the strength to have it out with Polly. I might have another attack."

Polly had stuck in a sheet of paper on which she had written, "Pete's suspicions were correct, but they remained suspicions which he kept to himself. The fact that he did is rather a mystery to me.

Was it only because he was afraid of another heart attack? We often had words about other things, usually banal domestic matters. It was on that morning that my affair with Maeda began, brief though it was. We did it half undressed on the floor in the kitchen. I must admit that the fear of Pete's discovering us heightened the excitement of it. Maeda was so innocent in spite of his age. He was worried about my having a child. I was fifty-six.

"The sad thing was that meetings were hard to arrange. We didn't dare do it in the kitchen again because Pete had asked me why Maeda had stayed so long that morning. I had managed to satisfy him with a story about sewing on a loose button for Maeda and having to search for the right-colored thread, which was light blue like his jacket, a garment I knew well. It's funny how one knows people's clothes as well almost as one knows them. So my lover and I met on shopping mornings when he was free. We went to a little hotel in the town that catered for such rendezvous. It was a beastly place, not all that clean: the *tatami* mats were shabby and they smelt musty. We were never in the hotel more than an hour, often less. These clandestine assignations went on for two and a half years when they were brought to a sudden end. While we were dressing one morning in the hotel Maeda suddenly said, 'Thank you very much for teaching me. I get married next month. I send you invitation.'

"'Can't we meet again here?'

"'Better not.'

"I sobbed all the way home and forgot to do the shopping. Maeda had simply used me for practice lovemaking so that he'd know how to make love properly when he got married. I must admit, though, that I enjoyed giving the lessons; it's fun instructing the innocent. I also think that he wanted to do *it* with a foreigner for the experience. Many Japanese are curious to know what a foreigner is like.

"When I got home, Pete noticed I'd been crying. I pretended to be feeling unwell and took myself up to bed in the spare room, locked the door and wept."

A few pages later came Pete's description of Maeda's wedding, which was held in the tourist hotel: "The absurdity of the modern Japanese wedding is beyond belief. First there is a Shinto marriage ceremony only attended by the families and very close friends. It was an honor, I suppose, for Polly and me to be invited to it. It was held in a chapel in the hotel exclusively used for weddings. A lot of mumbo-jumbo was muttered by the berobed priest in a high black lacquered hat and then came the exchange of saké cups between the bride and the bridegroom—she dressed in a kimono and wig, he in ill-fitting morning dress (hired, of course). Then followed the reception during which a Western-style meal was served and speeches were made. The bride and the groom sat dumb and glum at the top table with the go-between, who was responsible for arranging the match. They looked as if they were about to be executed. Halfway through the couple left the room to return in different clothes: she in a Western wedding dress and he in a dinner Jacket—also ill-fitting, also hired, no doubt.

"We all had to make speeches. Mine wasn't understood as I spoke in English after saying *o-medito* (congratulations); I said, 'Maeda-san has been my student for three years. I am sure his wife will find him as diligent a husband as I have found him a student.' Polly made a complete ass of herself. She went up to the microphone, blurted out, 'Congratulations!' and then broke down into tears and with a handkerchief to her face returned to our table. 'Weddings always get me that way,' she told me afterwards. 'You didn't break down at our wedding,' I reminded her. 'That was different,' she replied. After this ridiculous outbreak of emotion by Polly, which I may say, greatly embarrassed me, there followed the cutting of the many-tiered cake, most of which was made of cardboard, and the candle ceremony. The latter involves the bride and groom going from table to table, and after bowing reverently lighting the candle on each table. A ludicrous modern innovation, which the Japanese find touching. 'We don't do this in the West,' I told my neighbor, who didn't understand, of course. One gives money, not presents, at a Japanese wedding, and the amount depends on the nearness of one's relationship to the bride or the groom. I wanted to give 5000 yen. Polly insisted on giving 20,000 yen. 'That's over eighty pounds,' I told her. 'Never mind. He's been so good to us,' she said. I gave in, not without regret though. I must add in fairness that in return as it were for one's gift each guest gets a present—an illustration of the Japanese addiction to *quid pro quos* At this wedding every guest got a lacquered tray, not worth 20,000 yen."

Polly wrote: "The wedding was awful. It was, I knew, the end of any sensual pleasure I'd ever have. We were so isolated. The locals were shopkeepers, fishermen or farmers. There was no possible successor to Maeda among the hotel staff. Now and then Maeda called to see us. Once when he and I were sitting side by side in the kitchen having coffee, I put my hand on his thigh, fairly high up. He took hold of my hand and placed it on my lap as if returning something to its proper place. 'That finish,' he said.

"Then followed empty years. Some days Pete and I hardly exchanged a word. We followed our routine which became automatic. It might be wondered at this point why I married him. I did so because he was a dashing young officer and to get away from my mother, with whom I never got on. She never forgave me for not being a boy."

Pete's next piece of travelogue was about the planting, the weeding and the harvesting of rice. Not uninteresting, the account went into these stages, which included the festivals in detail. He must have studied the cultivation of Japan's principal crop carefully. I didn't read it all as turning over several pages by mistake I came upon my name and Pete's description of my visit:

"A friend of some old friends of Polly's spent the weekend. He's some printer fellow and called Jeremy Cottrell. Unmarried and overweight—*one of those,* probably; nevertheless he behaved fairly well, and seemed to know the basic duties of a guest. He brought a bottle of Chivas Regal, paid for drinks at the hotel and on his last night gave us dinner. Polly wheedled 20,000 yen out of him pretending she'd forgotten her purse when they went shopping. Ha! Ha! He's on an expense account for sure, so £80 means nothing to him. He'll get it off the firm. Both Polly and I were very courteous to him and hospitable. We took him swimming—he swam like a woman—and to Ise and Toba. Hope he doesn't descend on us again. Don't think he will. He'd be afraid of getting touched again. Good riddance!"

Polly wrote: "How impossible he'd become! He hated having guests, loathed putting himself out the tiniest bit, and disliked 'wasting money on them.' He says, 'Polly wheedled 20,000 yen out of him,' but Pete put me up to it. By this time I had got into a state of complete apathy. I realized that one can be more lonely with someone than when one is alone."

I looked up. A waiter was standing by me. "You like not?" he asked. I had been too absorbed to eat more than one of the chops. I rapidly finished the other, now cold, and ordered a slice of Black Forest cake—forbidden food, but it was Saturday. Walking back to my kennel, I mused about Pete's book and Polly's comments and confessions. I decided that it might be publishable if it were written as a novel. Much more could be made of Polly's affair with Maeda, who could play a bigger part in the story. Cottrell could be brought in too. Polly's lie about her purse (it being his idea rather than hers) provided another side to her character, a side which could be expanded. When a relationship breaks down one partner is never entirely to blame. There are always faults on both sides. The story could become one of cut and thrust; one of the thrusts being Polly's success in persuading Pete to quadruple the wedding gift to Maeda. Why did Pete, the monster martinet of whom she was afraid, give in over this? Pete's book with Polly's comments contained enough juicy ingredients for a novel. A novelist needs a germ, and hints, and gaps for his imagination to fill. But who would write it? Polly couldn't. She'd be too biased. I decided that I would write it and call it "Polly and Pete," It's good to start with a title.

John Haylock was born in Bournemouth, England, and educated at Aldenham School in France and at Pembroke College, Cambridge University. During most of World War II he was a liaison officer with the Greek Army. He has taught in Baghdad and Tokyo and traveled extensively. From 1965-1969 he wandered in Asia, Egypt, Morocco and Europe and came to rest in Cyprus for five years. In 1984 he retired from his university post in Japan but returns to visit in Japan each autumn. Mr. Haylock writes short stories, novels, reviews and articles. Best known in Great Britain, his writing reflects his erudition, good humor and the breadth of his travels. Over the years several of his stories have appeared in SSI.

"My being French creates a solidarity between us, almost a complicity."

The Boss

BY JANOU WALCUTT

WE are fortunate. As soon as the crocuses appear, we can creep out of the house, unfold our bodies stiffened by winter, sprawl in our garden chairs and let our eyes feast on the frothy green of the lawn without at the first fragrant insufflation of anticipated languor feeling harassed by the imperative necessity of mowing that lawn or pierced by the guilt of not mowing it. In this we enjoy an inestimable privilege: we are liberated from the enslavement of lawns. In our civilization, which is as surfeited as it is deprived, this luxury, cherished survivor of bygone days, seems to us almost equally shameful and precious. With the trembling intensity of the wine lover opening his last bottle of Mouton Rothschild 1953, we savor its fragile and delicate bouquet.

Every week or so, a troupe of gardeners glides from the wings onto our lawn and performs. In a graceful ballet, five or six chunky but nimble men pirouette around bushes, execute pliés, relevés and entrechats along the flowerbeds. They eventually cut the grass, the fresh and elusive scent of which mingles innocently with the nauseating emanations of the mechanical mower.

This mower is, assuredly, the gardener's mechanical Pompadour. Lovingly, in turn, they mount and ride her in virile delight. But just as the satiated lover flies to new conquest, inconstant, each rider of this faithful companion abandons her in a corner, useless, forlorn, still trembling, gasping, unsatisfied.

This infidelity is in fact a little strategem which permits the workmen to chew the fat or smoke a cigarette behind the big oak tree, while the Boss, reassured by the familiar sound of his team at work, can devote himself to surveying the next lawn and detailing the choreography of his next performance.

When I say the Boss *hears* the noise of the mower I may speak somewhat too confidently, for the Boss, our Portuguese gardener Alfonso de Alvarez, is deaf or nearly deaf. Some sounds, such as the clatter of working tools, the town siren announcing lunchtime for the team, the rustling of the monthly check in the customer's hand, reach him, but human voices penetrate his reluctant eardrum with difficulty, regardless how eager Alfonso is to hear.

Alfonso's team is a pure national unit, durably, perennially Portuguese. The individuals change but the nationality stays. Mother Portugal must be jealously sequestering her gardeners and their desendants. During all these years, among all these swarthy ambassadors to our Long Island lawns, not one seems ever to have seen a plant or a blade of grass before his arrival.

We have to accept the fact that Alfonso, too, is a gardener in name only, and his imported team continues with unyielding fidelity to uproot and cut down precious plants while they cherish and cultivate the dandelions. After all, the notion of "weeds" is very arbitrary; our astonished dandelions, thus pampered, glow in the emerald green of our lawn in golden clusters of defiant beauty.

None of the gardeners speak any English, except for the incantatory confident yet elusive "OK" with which they propitiate the strange and threatening American world around them. It is attentive, courteous, defensive, yet rarely reassuring.

Shepherding his hardy alien flock, Alfonso stands the undisputed

Chief, the *patron*. While their heads are bent over the ground, his eagle eye scans the trees, the birds, the horizon. His gait is proud, swinging, assured—pelvis forward, feet turned out in a perfect right angle, he marches over the ground as if he owned it. Alfonso stands out from his team in spite of his small size. His prestige springs from his "conversations" with his customers. Alfonso speaks English or a sort of "Portuglish" more mimed than spoken. Since Alfonso is deaf, his clients imagine that they have to deliver a loud torrent of words, to which Alfonso answers with a consummate artistry of sounds and motions. The authoritative gesture with which he seizes a rebellious azalea or snatches a tuft of grass suspected of perfidious languor puts him at center stage. His expressive mimes are accompanied by an uninterrupted flow of gutteral sounds. Since the words are not Portuguese, his men are dazzled by his virtuosity, not doubting for an instant that the Boss is expressing himself in English. They cannot help pausing for a moment to admire the performance, their mouths half open, their arms on the handles of their tools, their hats pushed away from brows that never get tanned. As for the customers, they cannot hear English in the staccato fusillade of Alfonso's delivery and are convinced that they are hearing pure Portuguese. They nod approval frantically in order to arrest the flow and escape their subordinate roles. Alfonso, once more emerging from such a difficult confrontation, does not doubt for an instant that he indeed possesses the magical key to this hermetic language. He accepts for a moment the silent admiration of his men who watch him move in this bilingual universe with such mastery; then, with a noble gesture of the hands, he sends them back to their assignments.

Alfonso de Alvarez is really a chief. Alfonso and I communicate very well, although our understanding does not rest heavily on the use of hearing. Alfonso can read the English words better on my French lips and I can recognize his English words under their Portuguese intonations. For Alfonso, I am just like him, a foreigner in America. My being French creates a solidarity between us, almost a complicity. When we "talk" it is Americans who almost become the foreigners, and we become virtually fellow countrymen, or so he thinks. We have carried our connivance even to the point of planting garlic and tomatoes near the formal roses, an audacity unheard of in this area where the lawn is queen and the vegetables undesirable commoners.

If this acceptance of a rustic familiarity may cost me a mite of the deference generally accorded to the mysterious and inscrutable employer, it brings me the recompense of the human warmth and solidarity that embraces the members of one's family after a heavy snowfall. Alfonso will drop by our house and dig out the driveway to liberate our car; if the weather gets cold, he comes to split a few logs and makes sure we have plenty of wood stacked in the cellar. When the lawns of the neighborhood no longer require his care, he comes to repair our collapsing fence and cement the flagstones and bricks that are always being dislocated by the winter frosts. We are the only people to benefit thus from Alfonso's varied talents; or, perhaps I should say, we are the only ones who prefer to have our fence mended by Alfonso, even if it is somewhat askew, and our bricks cemented by him, even if their alignment is a bit whimsical.

The warmth and solidity of our relationship was crowned one day with a bottle of quasi-muscatel wine; this was not any old bottle of wine, but a bottle containing a reddish gold fluid made by the very hands of Alfonso—yes—a wine "Mis en bouteilles à la proprieté de Alvarez." What a fine day it was, the day he brought this precious flask. Together, we sipped the unorthodox nectar. Our friendship was sealed forever on that day. Alfonso managed to hear real words coming from my mouth, which he repeated with delight. I was also able to make out a number of phrases that he articulated with utmost care. We had a feast of communication. Gesticulation became rather decorative than essential. We were moving bravely into new regions of language now, and thanks to the brilliant effect of the muscatel we were able to track four or five key words through the dense thicket of three languages: Portuguese, French, English. The strangeness of certain new words that he could read on my lips, through the intermediation of French, never ceased to delight him. His eyes were sparkling when he left, repeating: "You are welcome, you are welcome," an expression that had now come quite clear to him for the first time. Until now, he had failed to establish a connection between being well and coming since obviously he could not have come if he were not well.

From time to time, we have philosophic exchanges and beyond the severe limits of language, his deportment renders for me lessons in a natural wisdom that I respect and a cheerful disposition that I admire.

Even with his limited speech, Alfonso's arguments sometimes have such weight that I am left dumbfounded by them. For example, one fall we planted a hundred or so tulips and as many jonquil bulbs in the expectation of having in spring an early and lavish explosion of colors to signal the conquest of winter. Not a single flower, not a bud, not even a green stalk rewarded our faith. I was indigant at the greed of the wild rabbits and asked Alfonso what we could do, next fall, to stop them. Alfonso answered with the firm tone one uses to a heedless child: "Those rabbits have a right to live. If the Lord put them in your yard, He knew what he was doing." I must admit that I felt somewhat ashamed and contrite at my selfishness and lack of cosmic vision. So I distributed carrot tops and cabbage leaves in profusion. But the bulbs we continue to plant must still be their special delicacy for our yard still does not boast any considerable display of tulips. It has now become a parade ground of rabbits—the most densely populated parade ground of the plumpest rabbits in the whole area.

Alfonso's wisdom was less to my liking, one day, when I showed him a wasps' nest on our terrace. As I was telling him how dangerous it was because at every outdoor meal we had to watch every forkful lest it be seasoned with a live wasp, Alfonso answered with satisfaction: "What intelligent little creatures they are! Few people around here have their meals outdoors. The wasps know this and come here to you. They like it here and where the good Lord put them we must not touch them." I adamantly refused to submit to divine mysteries. To soften my insistence, however, I told Alfonso the family legend of the wasps that almost cost my brother his life.

Acknowledging the danger of a possible family allergy, Alfonso relented and came at night with a bag to take away the unwelcome wasps. I am afraid that this nest, tenderly gathered, landed in our neighbor's yard, for the next day I heard screams coming over the hedge and the voice of an alarmed paterfamilias shouting: "This is the first time we ever had wasps here." His cry was punctuated by gasps and frantic thuddings of a folded newspaper. Since our neighbors do not take their meals outdoors but in their screened porch, I wondered what wise explanation Alfonso would find in order to justify the presence of the wasps in their yard. Beyond that, moreover, I wondered how those poor people who do not have the extenuating circumstances of a family allergy were going to convince Alfonso to oppose the will of the Lord, especially when he knew so well who played God this time.

Nevertheless, I cannot help admiring in Alfonso his love for all living creatures. If he sees a fallen flower, he plants it above his ear, a coquetry which makes him look both innocent and roguish.

Alfonso is at peace with nature. In spring he whistles along with the birds; in summer, he lies under shady trees with the abandon of a trustful lion cub; when fall comes he caresses tenderly the first fallen leaf; at the first flurry of snow in icy weather he flails his arms across his body and stamps his feet against the cold. Alfonso is always cheerful and his smile is delightfully infectious. When we return from a trip to France, he welcomes us with a touching gaiety.

At a time when so many people are blasé or bitter or angry or desperate, it is a joy to have Alfonso's warm spontaneous welcome. He circles around us making a comprehensive examination to discover some lingering trace of the old world. He cries out, laughing: "So, I say, you have been on the other side. How was it there?" At the beginning of our friendship, I was slightly embarrassed at being able to take trips which I thought he could not afford and I would reply somewhat evasively. I know now that he could very well make this trip if he wanted to, but he prefers not to go back to a place where he no longer has family or friends. Alfonso is not envious. He has no jealous curiosity. He likes to think about the old world, distant, inaccessible, and hear about it. Neither does he want to see new countries. He is satisfied with the happy nostalgia of his memories. He knows that they are nestled comfortably within himself and would disintegrate if confronted with reality now.

Alfonso is a sage.

I admire the wise man in Alfonso, I admire the gardener less. His knowledge of gardening is feeble, not to say dangerous at times. In order to adopt modern methods, or what he thinks are modern methods, he occasionally tries to administer chemicals whose essential virtues and vices he does not begin to know.

So it was that one day we had on this account a misunderstanding that almost shattered our relationship. Our rose hedge is our special delight. In June, Alfonso brings his fullest attention to bear on this explosion of glory. None of his men are supposed to approach it. One spring, transported by a beautiful zeal, he decided to apply a special treatment and sprayed what seemed to be tons of insecticides on our roses, which were then in fullest brilliance. In less than a week the leaves started to wither, the branches to dry, and of our darling roses not one remained, not even a sickly bud. At the sight of our martyred beauty, we took our courage and spoke to Alfonso of our despair. Alfonso seemed more deaf than ever, but we did not let ourselves be mollified or disheartened. We told him, in no equivocal terms, not to "tend" our roses any more from now on. He was so sincerely contrite that we were embarrassed for having been so hard on him.

The next morning at dawn an unusual sound got us out of bed. From the window of our bedroom we saw Alfonso squarely poised on his robust calves directing a powerful and methodical spray of the same stinking deadly insecticide on our wounded and miserable roses. We rushed down to his side and stopped his criminal arm. The night before, Alfonso had responded fully to our dismay but had completely missed its true cause. His good generous concern saw only the miserable roses but did not dream of blaming the chemical. On the contrary, if one ounce was good, now was the time to do something ten times better by using ten ounces in the same amount of water.

Alfonso tried to find some profound statement to sum up the situation but on that day the words did not come freely. "Your rose bushes are getting rusty because we have too much rain. With all our planes and bombs we give the Lord too much trouble. He no longer knows where to turn next." Alfonso mumbled a few more words but in his heart did not seem to be in it.

The roses languished for the rest of the summer but the insecticide cloud could not darken our relationship permanently. Things fell back into place thanks to a bottle of Beaujolais that we forced him to accept in exchange for another "Chateau Alfonso de Alvarez" that he had brought to us as a peace offering.

Shortly after the episode of the rose hedge, on a sultry July afternoon I was resting on the couch in the cool shade of the house and was beginning to doze over my book, when the sheltering big rhododendron just outside the windows startled me by moving. I rubbed my eyes thinking of a dream or a coming storm when, all at once, I made out the bulky shape of one of the gardeners. He was groping his way in under the heavy branches. I rejoiced at the conscientiousness of this worker. Usually the gardeners are content to nudge a dreamy or haphazard rake only over the part of the ground that can be seen from the front. This particular rhododendron, as a matter of fact, had lately seemed to be in trouble. Its leaves were turning yellow. Here, now, I thought, this man who appeared like the simpleton of the team is more thorough than the rest of them and is going to direct his efforts toward reviving our precious bush. As I was going to raise a hand to congratulate the man, I saw at my eye level, two feet from my head, a hairy hand holding what I could no longer doubt was an enormous penis. I was dumbfounded and foolishly hid my head under the pillow to make myself invisible. Confused at witnessing such a scene I did not dare make a move that would reveal my presence and embarrass this halfwit and finally interrupt an action, alas, well under way.

The object, in itself, though of an extraordinary size, should not have appeared so monstrous and frightening to a mature woman who had long ago lived through the traumata of adolescence. I felt myself blush a bright scarlet as I reacted like a startled adolescent to the strange apparition of this anatomical explosion in such an unexpected place.

A week later, when I had almost forgotten this surprising episode, the same scene was displayed once more, although I was at a greater distance this time preparing lunch in the kitchen. Less surprised, less shocked, but more indignant, I decided to have a serious talk with Alfonso. I waited for the men to go to the next house and I accosted Alfonso on the front lawn. The subject was not easy to approach, though the situation demanded action in the name of propriety as well as in defense of the rhododendron's right to survive. Bravely and somewhat confusedly I told Alfonso that "this" was unacceptable. Alfonso agreed with me immediately and I felt relieved to get away with it so easily. I beat a prompt retreat to the front door. Alfonso, not used to such brief exchanges, pursued me and cut off my retreat. He seized the branches of the rhododendron vigorously and said: "I am going to give it a new food product. It will pep it up in no time. I think the Lord forgot to send us rain lately but he will soon remember." I saw that Alfonso was in one of his acute deafness days. I was tempted to give up right there and then, because not only was the subject delicate but I hated to complain about an employee behind his back.

I made a last half-hearted attempt and told Alfonso simply: "I have seen Pedro behind the rhododendron and I do not want to see him there anymore." All of a sudden, to my surprise, Alfonso understood everything. Obviously this was no news to him. He remained speechless for a while, scratching his head; then as if struck by a fabulous discovery he stared at me and said in a tone both incredulous and admiring: "So, then, *you* have seen Pedro's *THING!*" I could not deny the fact. I nodded a yes with a proper blush. Alfonso first grinned, then burst into resounding laughter. He slapped his thighs with delight. I was afraid that these outbursts would attract the attention of his men in the neighbor's yard, particularly Pedro's attention. Alfonso's explosive mirth began to grate on my nerves, but not as much as the sentence he repeated exasperatingly with changing intonations but with the same relish: "So, then, now you have seen Pedro's *THING!*"

Nevertheless, with his mouth split to his ears, his ringing laughter, Alfonso suddenly appeared to be like an eternal character out of a Brueghel canvas or of an old lithograph for an old edition of Gargantua and Pantagruel. With the twig of wisteria cascading from his ear, his ringing laughter seemed so direct, so natural, so healthy, that my initial shock gave way to tolerance, then amusement. I had to make an effort not to burst out laughing with him in my turn. How restful and honest such an attitude was. I could not help thinking about the nature of obscenity; how different his reaction was from the sordid decadent sexuality offered by films pretending to be erotic but, in fact, dribbling only sadism and sadness.

When Alfonso stopped laughing he did not know what to say. He tried to mumble some sensible words but had to stop to slap his thighs once more. The "thing" of Pedro was obviously a subject of admiration and discussion for the whole team and it happened that now, though unwillingly, I had shared the confidence. My silence was probably frustrating for Alfonso for he seemed almost to expect some expression of appreciation on my part, as if no one could have been privileged enough to see Pedro's *thing* and not wonder at such a rare marvel.

I stopped Alfonso short in the middle of the sentence which I had now heard for the nth time, establishing my complicity. I gathered my self-control and with dignity and perhaps excessive severity I declared without flinching: "Alfonso, see to it that such a situation does not occur any more." Alfonso immediately controlled his exploding laughter. He put his hand in front of his mouth to check himself. He took the twig of wisteria off his ear out of embarrassment or respect or perhaps in deference to the seriousness of the situation which he now grasped.

His expression changed and his face blanched. I realized that he was in the throes of painful conflict. He swayed from one foot to the other, pulled up his loose pants in a touching attempt to look dignified. He raised his hands in a gesture of helpless fate. On the one hand I was the lady of the big house responsible for the largest amount of work for his team, therefore the "BOSS" (and Alfonso has an acute sense of hierarchy); on the other hand *he* is the Boss too, for his men the only *patron*. Alfonso had his pride as a chief, as a Portuguese, and as a man. He was the male. Pedro was one of his own workers, a fellow countryman chosen by him, and he was a male to boot and had given proof of it. A woman should not dictate the law on a question of such gravity. I could feel that Alfonso was not going to capitulate but was going to deliver, for my instruction, some words of profound wisdom. Perhaps he was going to come up with such an audacity as: "If the Lord put Pedro and his *thing* in your path, He knew what he was doing."

Alfonso coughed to clear his throat. To my great surprise he came close to me with his fist raised and asked me: "Have you not seen on television the 'social troubles' as they call them?" I nodded, not knowing where he was leading and, under cover of a responsive smile, retreated a couple of steps from his threatening stance. I had never seen Alfonso de Alvarez frowning before. He, in turn, came forward one step, put his fists on his hip, raised his chin and demanded with an almost roguish tone: "Has Alfonso de Alvarez any 'social agitations' in his crew?" Alfonso seemed to be putting me through calculated interrogation. Docile, I moved my head from right to left in sign of negation.

"Do you know why Alfonso does not have any social troubles?" Alfonso drew back a step so as to better relish my perplexity, for I hesitated in confusion, not knowing what he was up to. He repeated his question less sternly and, as if softened by my ignorance, replaced the twig of wisteria over his ear. Alfonso seemed to want an answer or was he only playing cat and mouse knowing too well that he would catch me in the end. My mind rapidly sorted a kaleidescope of explanations for the Olympian calm that reigned on Alfonso's somewhat hangdog crew, but I realized that my socio-liberal explanations would not be warmly appreciated. Prudently, I abstained.

The moment was electrical. In spite of my expression of total helplessness, I felt Alfonso was getting impatient. "Why, tell me, why?" Alfonso demanded words, not merely gestures of ignorance. Therefore I merely complied: "Alfonso, I do not know." Alfonso sensed that triumph was within reach. He could now show his magnanimity and condescended to explanations. "Listen to me, Alfonso de Alvarez has his men under control and that is why they don't get out of line." With an ample gesture of his extended arm Alfonso showed me the perfect rectitude of that line. He suddenly turned back toward me and demanded point blank, practically under my nose, "Why do Alfonso's men not get out of line?" Another question! I had thought I had heard the end to them. I had to admit that I still did not know the answer.

Alfonso de Alvarez threw back an imaginary mane of hair. He struck his breast and looking me straight in the eye to discover, at last, a sign of admiration, said: "It is because Alfonso de Alvarez is just. He knows his duty. With their lunches, Alfonso gives his men a good bottle of wine. It makes the blood rich. They work hard, my men, but mark my word, lady, my men are real men, they are not mannikins, THEY HAVE TO PISS."

I gulped and tried to assimilate this indisputable fact with all the objectivity I could muster.

Alfonso seemed satisfied by my confusion and the brutal effect of this overpowering revelation on a feeble female, even if she considered herself the *Boss* of the property.

Alfonso pulled up hard on his sagging, beltless, braceless, baggy trousers with a swift gesture of virile confidence. He raised his chin. *He* was the real *Boss*: He was a MAN.

Leaving him in his frozen statuesque pose of noble avenger, I tried to beat a discreet retreat toward the house. But Alfonso did not want me to get away with it so easily. He grabbed my arm with an iron grip: "If not, if not, lady, what would happen?" For Heaven's sake, I thought, at a loss, another question. Has he lost his mind? He was staring at me with wild intensity, as if possessed. I began to shiver. Did he take himself for the matador on the verge of plunging for the ultimate thrust? I had never seen him like this before. Seen from such a close angle, his face practicaly touching mine, a Goyaesque grimace distorting his solid features, he looked like a completely different person. The answer to that new question must have been very different from the comic one that came irrepressibly to my mind. The answer he was going to let me hear must have been frightening, since he was now looking right and left suspiciously. In a whisper kept under control with effort as if the subject were a tragic and dangerous secret ready to explode, he said:

"If not, if not lady, Alfonso de Alvarez, the Revolution, he would have it on his arms." He looked inspired, his eyeballs upwards, his nostrils pinched (hissing a strange hooting). He presented to me in a dramatic gesture his two muscular arms as if they were still trembling from the weight of a calamity falling from a hostile sky. With a repressed sob, he entrusted me once more with this awesome prophecy: *"THE REVOLUTION, THE REVOLUTION,* lady, would be here!"

I had to agree to that. Heavens! History had witnessed revolutions exploding for less than that.

Born in France and graduated from Lyon University, Janou Walcutt taught in Lyon and Paris prior to becoming Director of the Benjamin Franklin Library in Paris. She has also taught French literature on the college level in the USA. She now devotes all her time to writing and painting. Her short stories are published in France and the USA and her paintings are in French and American collections. Presently she is in the USA.

"We need knowledgeable men like you with
a firm grasp of tradition to preserve
our age-hallowed culture."

The Senator's Suit

BY ROBERT H. BROWN

HE stood in front of the little unfinished church, his eyes glued on legendary figures on a hut across from the mission-station. He flexed his slender, ebony-black arms. His graceful fingers, like those of a pianist's, groped restlessly for his glasses in a breast-pocket. He put on his steel-rimmed glasses and shot a scrutinizing look at the legendary figures again. Somehow these figures reminded him of some he had read about in classical mythology, but he could not exactly recall which ones. His attention was diverted by the bleating of goats standing along a public footpath, chewing the cud. He was startled by a noise emanating from the northernmost section of the town. A rabble of boys and girls and stray goats and sheep came bolting down, like lightning, to the southernmost section of the town, yelling and shouting, brown-striped with red dust, all mixed in the same swirling stampede. Then he looked at his unfinished church again. Where would he get the money to buy construction materials to finish his church? Then there were taxes and his son's tuition fees to be paid. The Good Lord will provide, he thought. As all this ran through his mind, Nyeswoa, his trusted friend, crept up surreptitiously behind him and tapped him on the shoulders. He was startled, as if Nyeswoa were intruding into his private world of thought.

"Good morning, Teacher," Nyeswoa said.

"Good morning, my friend," Teacher said. "You startled me," he went on, smiling. His face wrinkled beautifully when he smiled. He coughed lightly and beckoned to Nyeswoa to sit down.

Both sat in chairs of braided raffia. Presently, Nyeswoa produced two kola nuts, a gourd of palm wine, and a jar of ground pepper from a raffia bag.

"A token of our continuing friendship," Nyeswoa said, offering Teacher a kola nut.

"Why do you always carry kola with you? You know I can always offer you a kola," Teacher said.

"I always carry kola because our women these days are not what they used to be. You know kola not only drives away hunger, it is also a good antidote for malaria. And it also kindles and reinforces our relationships with our kith and kin, and our ancestors and gods," Nyeswoa said, laughing. He rose, stroked his beard and sat down again. The chair gnashed and shuddered beneath his weight.

"It isn't this type of kola that is used as an antidote for malaria; it's bitter kola," Teacher put in.

"You're right," said Nyeswoa. "But the regular kola has many uses. One of the uses is that it helps to identify practitioners of witchcraft. So you see, I carry kola nuts with me just in case someone commits a crime involving some witchcraft and denies it, I can produce one immediately. We can then recite a certain formula, slit the kola with a razorblade, and give it to the alleged culprit. If he's foolish enough and eats it instead of confessing, he will die a horrible death," Nyeswoa continued, laughing and slapping his robust thighs with his thick, powerful hands. He spoke the Grebo language beautifully. His teeth were stained from eating kola constantly. His eyes, as if from incessant weeping, were bloodshot.

"You're a knowledgeable man, Nyeswoa," Teacher said, "but I do know all about the uses of kola."

"I am a knowledgeable man indeed. I suppose that's why I want to succeed the High Priest of this chiefdom," Nyeswoa went on stroking his head with its pronounced, receding hairline.

"We need knowledgeable men like you with a firm grasp of tradition to preserve our age-hallowed culture," Teacher said.

Although Teacher was a university graduate, he was never really cut off from his tribal links and rich African heritage. Some of his urban counterparts were invariably ashamed of their tribal roots, but he had no such illusions. Most of his classmates read law and occupied positions of leadership in the government. But he followed in his father's footsteps and became a minister of the gospel and teacher. He ran a mission school singlehandedly. Tuition fees were voluntary and, when necessary, were often paid in five or ten points of rice. But he was already proud of two of his products: one was the Paramount Chief's son and the other was his own. Both were now secondary school students in Harper. Because of his patience, understanding, and ability as a teacher, he was affectionately and popularly known as Teacher. He bore everyone's burden and cares with unparalleled fortitude. This, at times, made him morose. However, his wife and friend often gave him the ballast needed in his moments of trials and tribulations.

"I've heard that the District Commissioner wrote the Paramount Chief that our taxes are long overdue. You know that's not true. The D.C. is just doing that to give himself ample time to collect his commissions. You should demand a salary for reading his letters to the Paramount Chief. If I could read and write, I'd ask the P.C. to make me the Chiefdom's Chief Clerk."

"I do it in the name of the Lord," Teacher said.

"Yes, but we say God helps those who help themselves. Remember you have your son's tuition fees and taxes to pay. Besides that, you run a school and get virtually nothing for doing it."

"The Good Lord will provide," Teacher persisted.

In a tree on the outskirts of the town an owl hooted.

"Did you hear what I've just heard?" Nyeswoa asked.

"No. What was it?"

"The hooting of an owl in broad daylight. That's an evil omen. And look right in front of us. There is another omen."

Teacher shot a look in front of them. Below a stump of a breadfruit tree a millipede had burrowed itself, somersaulting into the earth. Although Teacher was not superstitious, he found something uncanny about his clansmen's interpretations of signs and natural phenomena.

"Something dreadful is going to happen in this clan," Nyeswoa said. "I understand the High Priest hasn't been feeling well lately. He has even sent for his son who works in a gold mine in Tchien. This is probably the seventh time he has sent for him. Every time his son arrives, he recovers. I suppose he wants to persuade the Elders to have his favorite son succeed him. The young man should look forward to brighter days. His father is very wealthy—what with all his cattle, huge cocoa farm, wives, and beautiful daughters—his son should have a bright future. And as old as the *Bodior* is, he still likes wearing a coat-suit to see the D.C. The funny part about the whole thing is that he hardly ever wears the insignia of his office around his ankle. What's happening to our clan, to the norms and values established by our forefathers? And you're the fool to lend him your suits."

"I do it in the name of the Lord. Besides, he wants to buy the black suit a senator-friend gave me last year during a church convocation in Harper. The poor man and his wife went to Europe on a health trip for over a year now. He and his wife always accommodated me. Now I have to look for new living quarters for the forthcoming convocation. Besides, the suit is too big for me. It'll fit the *Bodior* perfectly."

"Let him give you a cow for the suit. That will help you finish your church. I wonder what will his eldest son do with all that wealth when the old man dies," Nyeswoa continued, beaming a baleful look on the ground and crunching a piece of kola. "I don't know how that man ever became the *Bodior*. He was a playboy in his youth. He had a lover in almost every family in this town. But he met his match in Nyema, who ran behind him with a cutlass for having an affair with Nyema's young bride. Nyema should have chopped off his head."

"That sort of wishful thinking is ungodly," said Teacher, clasping his hands in an attitude of prayer.

"Pray for me. That's why we're friends. I can't pray. Every night when I close my eyes to pray, the memory of my young wives distracts my sense of concentration. I don't want these young men who've just returned from Firestone and the gold mines in Tchien to take my young wives as lovers. I don't like their *kwii* ways."

"You're worrying over nothing. I think you would solve that problem if you had married only one wife. The Lord meant it that way."

"That's one law I don't mind breaking. Besides, marrying as many wives as one can afford has been our tradition for years. Tradition is hard to break. It's all right for you because you're educated."

"It makes no difference whether you're educated or not. The Lord meant it that way."

"If you insist, I would argue that the Lord never meant it that way. Look at some of those people you preach to us about in the *Bible*, God's own book. Some of them had several wives and concubines. What's the name of that man who was said to be a very wise man?" Nyeswoa asked, stroking his head.

"Solomon."

"Yes, Solomon. Now that man had several hundred wives and concubines. The thing I really don't understand about God is why did he give Solomon all that wisdom when Solomon had all those women? The same thing applies to the *Bodior*. Not only is he a knowledgeable man, but he's blessed with wealth as well. And that man was a playboy in his youth. I really can't understand God sometimes. By the way, where's your wife?"

"She's in the house. It's Saturday, so she's cleaning up," Teacher said.

"I really don't think ill of the *Bodior*. He has served the clan in his own little weak ways. In fact, I think he has done really well," Nyeswoa said. He looked mournfully at the breadfruit stump again. The millipede had burrowed itself completely into the earth.

"I'm glad you wish the High Priest well," Teacher said.

"But that sign may be foreshadowing the death of the District Commissioner himself. That man is getting richer every year. The rogue!"

"He's doing his job, and he also wants to feather his own nest," Teacher put in.

"I don't care! I wish he were dead before he began to feather his nest," said Nyeswoa. He roared with laughter, his prominent navel inflating like a balloon. When he laughed, it seemed as if the essence of his being depended on it.

"Is your tax ready? I understand a soldier, the tax-collector's forerunner, arrived yesterday," Teacher said.

"I only have half of it. I don't know when that Lebanese businessman will return from Monrovia. I want to sell my cocoa and palm oil. That potbelly of a soldier arrived yesterday. We were lucky there were some men in town, or else he would slaughter some poor man's goat and eat half of it before the poor man returned from his farm. That's why the other clan nearly beat a soldier to death last year. Now soldiers don't fool around with anyone in that clan any longer."

"Yes. I agree that these soldiers are brutal and ungodly at times. but that doesn't mean that they should be treated like beasts," Teacher said.

"If they act like beasts, they will be treated like beasts. How else would you treat a dog that bites for no good reason? Something has got to be done, or else these damned soldiers and tax collectors will hound us out of our own clan," Nyeswoa said, rising. "I'll see you."

He lumbered at incredibly quick trots, crunching a piece of kola nut and stroking his prominent navel. He was a cheerful man whose massive frame belied his childish mirth. Teacher watched him fade into the distance. His loud guffaws echoed in Teacher's ears. A fine specimen of a man, Teacher thought.

Then Teacher rose from the chair of braid raffia, walked a few yards under the eaves of his palaver-hut and dropped himself very comfortably into a hammock. He was a pensive man, often sinking himself into a maze of deep thoughts. Thoughts of God and his family.

"What's the matter, honey?" his wife asked with great solicitude, placing her right hand on his for a moment and then caressing it.

"Just thinking," Teacher said.

"Are you worried about Jimmy's tuition fees?" she asked.

"Well, yes. And then there's the tax to be paid soon. If we deduct the tax from what we have, then Jimmy's tuition fees will be affected. And Jimmy's tuition fees have to be paid if he's to sit for his final examination. That's what he wrote in his last letter to us. And, dear Lord, I want to finish roofing the church before the farmine season steps in. But there isn't enough money to buy zinc and cement."

"The Good Lord will provide," Teacher's wife said, almost mechanically.

"You're beginning to sound like me. I only pray that that Lebanese business tycoon returns to Yorkeh soon. Perhaps we can pawn something."

"He's a good pawnbroker, but my sewing machine got wrecked in his store the last time we pawned it. I would be doing some sewing if the machine were working. Christmas is right around the corner, and these women are hounding me out of my mind for their *lappa* suits."

"Talking about suits. Where's that black suit the senator gave me during the last convocation?"

"It's in the trunk. Why?"

"Please brush and iron it. The *Bodior* wants to buy it."

"Are you sure you want to sell that suit?"

"Yes. Besides, it's too big for me. It will fit the *Bodior* perfectly. My other black suit is still in a good shape," Teacher said, taking his *Bible* and zipping it open. As he read, he heard hoofbeats on the public footpath leading from the town to the mission-station. It was the *Bodior* and his son. His son led a cow by a rope round its neck. Teacher's mouth was agape with surprise.

"Good morning, Teacher," said the *Bodior*. His ankles were betasseled with tiny bells. He walked with awesome dignity, setting his ankle-bells ajingle. His starched loincloth rustled as he approached Teacher. He put aside his solemnity and sat on a goatskin mat in front of Teacher. He ran his left hand over a mop of gray, woolly hair. In spite of his old, scrawny hands and leathery skin, he was not altogether unprepossessing.

"I've come to buy the black suit," the *Bodior* said in a rather hoarse voice. "I have no money, but I'm offering a cow. You know this is the tax season, so times are hard."

"*Bodior*, God won't bless me if I took that cow in exchange for the suit. That cow is worth more than five hundred dollars, and that suit is probably worth only fifty dollars."

"It's mine to worry about. Besides, there's your unfinished church. You can kill the cow and take it to the butcher's shop for sale. I may be the High Priest, but I believe in God and I need His blessings, too."

"All right, *Bodior,* the suit is yours. By the way, I was told that you were ill. How are you now?"

"My son, I am no more as active as I used to be. Old age. I can feel it."

"We will keep you in our prayers. And don't worry—you'll live to be over a hundred," Teacher said. He called his wife to bring the suit. She brought it, her face ablaze with joy. In her hand something lay crumbled up.

"Here's the suit," said Teacher. "Your son can leash the cow to that breadfruit stump."

"Thank you, Teacher. Now I can see the D.C. in a dignified manner. I'm going to see him about the sacred objects his soldiers desecrated last year when they came to collect taxes." He gave the suit to his son and rose from the goatskin mat with the help of his cane.

When the *Bodior* and his son were a few yards away, Teacher's wife tapped him on the shoulder and said, "This is what I got from a pocket of the coat."

"A five-hundred dollar note!" Teacher exclaimed.

"Yes, the Good Lord has provided everything to finish the church and meet all our financial obligations. And you ought to be ashamed of yourself, worrying about paying Jimmy's tuition fees and taxes."

"Yes, the Good Lord has provided everything to finish the church and pay all our bills. Do you think the senator placed the money in the pocket of the coat intentionally?"

"I don't know, but God works in His mysterious ways—His wonders to perform," said Teacher's wife.

"I think we should return the money to the senator," Teacher said.

"I thought you said they went to Europe on a health trip."

"Oh, yes," Teacher said.

"Well, in that case the Good Lord has provided it."

"We could use the money and then inform the Senator about it when he returns from Europe. I'm sure he'll approve of the good use to which we put the money."

"I'm sure he will," said his wife.

After the church service, the next morning, Nyeswoa visited Teacher. He wore a mournful, guilt-ridden look. "Bad news!" he said bluntly.

"What's the bad news?" Teacher asked, offering Nyeswoa a chair of braided raffia.

"*Bodior* died early this morning. It's strange. They said he woke up early this morning, bathed, and put on the black suit in readiness for his mission to the District Commissioner. Just as he was about to pick up his cane, he dropped dead."

"In the senator's suit?" Teacher asked.

"In the senator's suit," Nyeswoa said.

"But the drums have not sounded the message of his death. The other clans should be informed. Strange, isn't it? And he has died on a Sunday, too."

"The drums will send out messages as soon as the High Priest's successor is chosen. I came to get you to witness the ritual. Oh, my! The sun is getting unbearably hot," said Nyeswoa.

"It is, isn't it?"

"I wish I were a member of that family. I would be a good candidate for the office of the *Bodior*," Nyeswoa said, picking up a chair and following Teacher with apostolic devotion into the palaver-hut.

"Why would you want to become the *Bodior*? It is an office of great responsibilities."

"I know, but what you get on the side makes up for everything. Imagine! I would have the whole town of Yorkeh brushing my farm. I wouldn't even have to worry about meat and fish, let alone palm nuts, salt and pepper. That's enough to make anyone crave for that office."

"Is it?"

"Certainly," said Nyeswoa, opening his bag and pulling out a gourd of palm wine and kola nuts. "Palm wine is good for your eyes. If you drank palm wine in your youth, you wouldn't be wearing glasses today."

"A moderate amount of palm wine is good once in a while, I agree," Teacher said, taking the gourd of palm wine and swilling down several swigs.

"Perhaps palm wine is an exception," Nyeswoa said. "Even St. Paul drank it."

"It was St. Timothy, not St. Paul, who drank wine. St. Paul advised him to drink wine for medical reasons. He had a stomach complaint," Teacher continued.

"Well, you're the Teacher and Preacher. Anyway, it goes to show that I really listen to your sermons. Let's go witness the ritual in town," Nyeswoa said, rising and leading the way into town.

Now that the High Priest had died, the responsibility of selecting a new High Priest suddenly loomed before the elders of the clan. The ritual began with the usual hustle and bustle of the aftermath of harvest. Women with earthenware filled with fresh creek water whisked past each other, exchanging the latest piece of gossip. As the day rolled into the late afternoon, pre-festival and ritual activities seemed to reach their peak. Hens clucked in front of the palaver-hut perched neatly on a raised mound of dirt in the center of the town. On the outskirts of the town stood goats chewing the cud. In the background breadfruit trees billowed their hems to the ground. The dead *Bodior's* eldest son emerged from behind one of the breadfruit trees. Carrying a machete in his right hand, he moaned painfully as blood spurted from his left foot. He had, with a determination and courage, sliced off the small toe of his left foot. By this single act of defiance and self-mutilation, he had disqualified himself as the logical choice in the familial group for the office of the *Bodior*, for a prospective *Bodior* must not have the minutest vestige of physical deformity. His young brother, reputed to be endowed with special powers, was the next one in line. Teacher and Nyeswoa stood in the crowd. They were much concerned.

"Why did he do that?" Teacher asked, quite bewildered.

"He wants to follow the *kwii* ways and become rich," said a middlle-aged man,.

"That's true," Nyeswoa put in. "He wants to be a civilized man by returning to Firestone and Tchien to amass wealth and build big houses for his mistresses. Then he can become a big man. Maybe a D.C. or a senator. He can read and write."

"Fool! Beast of no land!" another elderly man said angrily.

"Our young men these days are good for nothing. This *kwii* business has gone to their heads," said Nyeswoa, curling up his lips in utter disgust.

"That's why they will die horrible deaths," said a sedate old lady, sitting on a footstool with sibylline serenity.

Meanwhile, construction workers were busy building a new home for the new *Bodior.* According to tradition, a High Priest's home had to be built and completed in twenty-four hours or less. Before noon, the house was ready for occupancy.

Then later that afternoon the ritual began. The men delegated to capture the prospective High Priest began their task. They pursued the dead *Bodior's* young son to the outskirts of the town. They struggled violently with him as an Elder slipped an anklet betasseled with tiny bells around his right ankle. Then the young *Bodior* sat solemnly and serenely on the ritual goatskin mat, the insignia of his office around his right ankle. Beside him lay the baton of his office with curved figurines of male heads. In front of him a ritual axe was ceremonially planted to forestall lightning.

The orator of the occasion—tall, massive, and superior— lumbered in front of the crowd, facing the *Bodior.* Then in a solemn, captivating tone he said briefly and succinctly:

"*Today you have been chosen as the Bodior not because you are the most handsome man in this clan.*" (Here the young girls giggled.) "*But because you're the next logical choice after your brother, the supposed vanguard in the familial group, disqualified himself. From this very moment the medicine of the clan is entrusted to your care. This means you are the eye of this clan. It means you will use the power of your office to forestall witchcraft and internecine tribal warfares.*

"*From experience we recall that by repeating a certain formula you exorcised an evil spirit from a woman who was bewitched and possessed. I must warn you that assuming the office of the Bodior is not idle. It is an office of great responsibilities. Use your sixth sense well, and may our ancestors guide you in executing the duties of your office. Reign supreme.*"

Suddenly the leaves of trees arched downward, foreshowing rain. In a few moments drums boomed. Soon clouds blanketed the azure sky. Thunder roared and rumbled. One could feel the very earth quake beneath him. Then the storm struck, and the clouds released torrents of rain, alleviating the infernal heat.

Born in southeastern Liberia, in 1945, Robert H. Brown proved an excellent student and received a scholarship from the Holy Cross Fathers to study at Stonehill College in Massachusetts, USA, where he earned a B.A. He worked as a Research Officer at the Ministry of Information, Cultural Affairs and Tourism in Monrovia before entering Howard University, USA, where he was awarded an M.A. He has also earned an M.A. in Language and Literature from the University of London and a Ph.D. from the University of Essex, England. In addition to writing, Dr. Brown has taught at the university level.

"Undaunted, I next invited my friends
to become members of a special
club that I was launching."

My Eyes Opened
in Hackney

BY OLIVE WINCHESTER

A friend once told me, "Your birthdate 5.10.1919 could be lucky.
The numbers double up; you are also a Libran—a balanced person."
But am I?

To answer that question I have set down some of the experiences
of my seven decades.

I was born on a Sunday in the Salvation Army Home in
Hackney, London, which makes me a Cockney. I belong to a
band of people who are reputed to be cheerful survivors.

At my birth, the doctor discovered that my feet were turned in.
Guy's hospital staff and splints soon set them right. But, although
the feet are serviceable they look distinctly odd. Also I tend to trip
up people because I cannot walk in a straight line. Our gym
teacher looked puzzled as she examined the feet, for I could not
master the graceful toeing and heeling of the marching style.

"Never mind," she said, "they don't show when you swarm up
the rope."

In my second decade it was discovered that I could run, albeit with a curious loping stride and I represented the school in the 100 yard race. By then I had become short-sighted and my glasses often slipped off my nose en route. The short sight handicap was discovered at the cinema.

Mother and I sat one night in the shilling seats, as a treat instead of the seven-penny ones in the front row. When the writing came onto the screen I said, "Mum, I can't read it."

"Of course you can," said Mother crossly, glaring at me. "I can." (Mother had superb sight until her death at ninety-five.)

I was not upset at being the only girl in the class wearing glasses because I was stage-struck at this time. Mother could not afford the dancing lessons, which often led to performing, so my friend Emily (who had shapely feet) and I arranged a song and dance act. Our friends were impressed. Emboldened by their praise we contacted the manager of the Lido dance hall and offered this gem to him.

"Are you in need of a cabaret act, in between dances?" I asked him. "Quite cheaply," I added as he hesitated. He scrutinized us thoughtfully. "I will give you an audition. Be here at ten o'clock next Wednesday morning."

We ran home, singing, dancing and shouting, "We'll be famous."

It was a pity, but Emily's mother forbade her to even "set a finger inside that Lido." Emily and I hastily trained our friend Stella who was willing to partner me. Her mother, like mine, was ignorant of our venture.

What a thrill it was! The dance band played just for us. We sang and cavorted with gusto in our gym slips. Afterwards the manager thanked us and said gravely, "We will let you know. We may be engaging some children to perform exercises here." He did not even take our names and addresses.

Undaunted, I next invited my friends to become members of a special club that I was launching named *The Order of the Twisted Tooth*. I was its President, Secretary and Committee of One. There were no fees and, as I enjoyed bookkeeping, I offered to save the members money for them, which they could withdraw at any time. All the friends enrolled. Our other activities were walking, and cycling if we owned or could borrow a bicycle. Stella and I cycled to Brighton and back in a day, a distance of eighty miles. I admit that we found sitting rather difficult for some days after this feat. The club members honored us with a feast of stale cakes from the local bakery. A large bag of these cakes could be bought for sixpence, enough to feed six girls well.

My having to leave school when I was fourteen-and-a-half years old was sad. It was necessary for me to add a few shillings to the household. My widowed mother had remarried and my stepfather, who was illiterate could only work as a laborer. His jobs were poorly paid and insecure. School days had to be left behind.

I especially missed our headmaster, a wonderful man who could make any subject interesting. Many Sundays he invited us top class girls to his home for tea and after tea he helped with our bookkeeping homework. He was an organist and choirmaster and introduced us to music. Above all he encouraged us to be proud of ourselves. "You all have the ability to succeed," he said.

His words gave me confidence when I applied for and was accepted for a cashier's job at Coulsdon. I cycled to work each morning, riding behind a cement truck, often hanging on to the tailboard chain. This warded off the bitter wind of the English winter. It was rather dangerous and one had to be alert if the truck stopped suddenly.

The work as a cashier was exacting, the hours long, but the company was fun. I was able to attend night school at the Croydon Polytechnic for shorthand and typing on the two nights the shop closed early. I also experienced my first romance at this job. D was the provision hand. From my cash desk I could gaze at him as he cut the bacon and wrapped it beautifully for the customers.

At sixteen, I began to save two shillings a week towards getting married. D was nineteen, which seemed old to me. My post office savings book showed one pound and eighteen shillings when the stage struck again. I spent the money on tap dancing lessons, and then changed my job to an office one with shorter hours. This enabled me to take courses in Spanish, English and Advanced Cooking at the Polytechnic. The tuition for all three courses was one pound for the whole year.

Real romance happened when I was seventeen-and-a-half. I met B. Even dancing was forgotten. It was the happiest time. Our pleasures were simple. We sang, laughed, talked, cycled and swam. We planned to marry when I was twenty.

In 1938, after Neville Chamberlain's claim of "Peace in our time," the political situation worsened as we expected. On September the third, 1939, at eleven in the morning World War II began. B and I met as the air raid sirens wailed; we sheltered under the porch of the *Swan and Sugar Loaf* public house. We were glad that our marriage was only thirteen days away.

We were married at 8:30 in the morning in the Methodist church by a racy army chaplain and afterwards we ate Welsh rarebit for our wedding breakfast at the local cookshop.

My third decade began with our life together in a flat at Tolworth. B brought Pat, his old terrier to live with us. I loved him too. Burst pipes that winter flooded the bedroom and stairs of the flat. We only laughed at discomfort. In the spring of 1940 we moved to a house in Chessington. In August, B was called up for service in the Royal Artillery. We had deliberately avoided talking about the separation that we knew was inevitable, now it was here.

Then the air raids began, Pat and I huddled together in the Anderson shelter as the bombs whistled down. Whenever I smell bacon frying, I remember how good it tasted after a night spent trembling in the shelter. And Pat drooled over bacon rind.

My job at that time was working the control office in an aircraft factory where gun turrets for planes were designed and manufactured. When the air raid sirens sounded in the day time, we donned tin hats and carried on working. Guards stationed on the roof of the factory alerted us when enemy planes were near. Then red, white and blue lights flashed, buzzers blared in the machine shop as the foreman hustled everyone out to the shelters. His language was extremely colorful to the stragglers. The raids were never so frightening shared in the company of those men, laughter rang out from the shelters.

B came home on embarkation leave in May, 1941, for a week. When he rejoined his regiment my thoughts alternated between the dread of seeing a telegram on the doormat and the firm conviction that a tragedy could not happen to us.

One glorious sunny day in July, 1942, I went rowing on the Thames with a friend. Afterwards I walked up the road to home, feeling relaxed and happy. The raids were less frequent, letters from B were optimistic. The key clicked in the lock, Pat came to meet me, I remember his smile and the wag of his plumy tail, I bent down to caress him. The yellow telegram was waiting. I read its bald statement. The pattern of my life had altered. Until dusk I sat in the garden. A friend called, took Pat and me into her home for the night.

The next morning I contacted B's brother. Together we journeyed to Croydon to break the sad news to his mother. Forty-six years afterwards I can still see her face as we embraced. I returned to work the next day and B's mother came to stay for a while. She cooked marvelous meals from the rations. She put aside her own grief in her concern for me. She was brave lady and I was so grateful for her company. The war was only halfway through.

Somehow one adjusts. I had become accustomed to the loneliness, I had been keeping the home ready for B's return. Now there was only Pat, and me.

I did not plan to marry again but I did want children. When V, who was an engineer in the experimental department of the works proposed, I accepted. We married in October, 1943. B's mother had encouraged me to re-marry. "You are too young to stay on your own," she said, adding, "the Boy would approve." She also came to the wedding.

Our son was born in August, 1944, in a Jewish hospital near Hampton Court Palace, in the middle of a flying bomb raid. I learned much about the Jewish religion during my stay there. I was known as the *gentile* woman and asked to open the letters for the Jewish mothers on their Sabbath. The opening of letters was considered work, which they were not allowed to do, they were allowed to read them though. I enjoyed my time in that hospital so much that I returned in August, 1946, to have a daughter.

Life with two children was busy, satisfying and different. It was a more mature happiness. Old Pat had died and a young Pat settled in his place. He was a clown, he jumped fences and was always laughing. He and the children loved each other. He died when he was only eight years old.

In 1951 we emigrated to New Zealand. Our fares were paid by the New Zealand governrnent, a house and a job were waiting for us. We sailed from Southampton on the Atlantis, confident that the venture would be of benefit to us all.

The fourth decade was full of new interests; we had found our niche. The children attended a school whose pupils came from many countries. V enjoyed the challenge of a job with interesting prospects. Over the years he was sent to Australia, Germany, Sweden, America and England. I was able to take classes at the Auckland University Extension. For years I was the student in the front row at lectures on Spanish, English, Philosophy and many others. I considered a loss of hearing was no reason for a withdrawal from learning. Then I began to write.

Life is never the same once the writing bug attacks. I was fascinated. First I joined a Workers' Educational Creative Writing course, then moved on to Penwomen's Club, and Playwrights' Association. Finally I was accepted into Women Writers' Society. This meant that I had actually seen my work in print and listened to it over the radio.

An added interest was the Auckland competitions. I watched the children's progress through the years in dancing, singing, drama and music. Many of those competitors are now world-famous. I became an enthusiastic patron of the arts. No longer did I aspire to be a performer.

In the fifth decade, after 17 years in New Zealand, I was able to visit England and my mother. She was 79 and as spry as ever, reading avidly. I rediscovered all my interesting relatives and friends. Then came the wrench of leaving them all. But I was also homesick for New Zealand, home and family.

I embarked on ten years of service to Lifeline. This work gave me insight to the sadness in people's lives, which on the surface appeared to be happy. I found that taking the night shift was a time when I could get very close to people. I learned also that to be a successful telephone counselor meant to listen, but not give advice, and to cease thinking of the problems when I left the Lifeline room. My own life was enriched by the Lifeline experience.

By the beginning of the sixth decade, both our son and daughter were married. Although V and I missed them, we felt a sense of freedom at being on our own again. We took over both their bedrooms for our hobbies.

When V retired we took a trip to England together. Most of our relations had died, except Mother who at 89 was still active, if a little vague. School friends were welcoming, it was especially good to see Emily of the dancing period.

When we returnd home, V and I planned a new kitchen system. Each day only one of us was to be responsible for meals. The kitchen person had to prepare, cook and wash up after meals. The other could sit and talk to the cook, but did not have to help. Therefore, on alternate days we had no chores to do and could devote that time to hobbies. The scheme worked perfectly. V gained a whole new range of skills. For me, there was not only extra time to write but also the supreme enjoyment of eating meals I had not cooked.

Another milestone was the day I received the University calendar in the post from my daughter. With it was a cryptic note which read, "Dear Mother, here is the number of the Liaison Officer. Good luck. See you soon." I was amazed. As a person without secondary schooling, how could I grasp tertiary education? J called and explained. "Just take a couple of English papers, they'll help with your writing. You needn't go beyond that point." I laughed, then said, "Great idea. Why not?"

Enrollment was exciting but when I sat in the lecture theater for the first time, I experienced a feeling of panic. I relaxed as the lecture on Chaucer began. I sensed that I was going to enjoy studying for a degree. Exams as well.

Before I began the B.A., Monday was just a washing day. Now, as a student, I caught an early bus to the University, went to a lecture, studied in the library, had lunch and joined in the lively discussions with students of all ages. In the evenings I studied at home, wrote essays and *swotted* for tests and exams. I was grateful to V and the kitchen plan for dinner was waiting when I came home late. And our meal time talks were stimulating too.

Life was vital, the years flew and the journeying through university, although hard work, was a real pleasure. On May 5th this year I was capped B.A. majoring in English and Art History. I still cannot believe it!

I left for England six days later. The Salvation Army Home, where I first opened my eyes, is there still. But my roots are not in Hackney. They are now transplanted firmly in New Zealand.

As I approach the end of my seventh decade, tap dancing has lured me again. The teacher welcomes mature students with interest. (The encounter with Emily re-awakened the urge ten years ago, but study was the top priority until 1988).

And study? Yes, I have already applied to begin a Masters' degree in 1989. One granddaughter will be a student at the same university.

As we have five grandchildren, I look forward to the eighth decade with the hope that sometime in the future I may realize another ambition, to be a great-grandmother.

I consider that I have been lucky to meet people who have loved and helped me to make my life a happy and interesting one. Many of these people are Librans and have personalities as balanced as a watchmaker's scales...I can only compare my personality with that of the irregular movement of a seesaw.

A graduate of the University of Auckland, Olive Winchester writes for adults and children. Her cheerful, positive outlook is evident in all her work; she is refreshing. Her story "Bequeath Me Your Genes" appeared in SSI No. 84.

"...having confirmed that the old man was drunk enough not to feel any pain, we set to work."

The Village Doctor

BY WALE OKEDIRAN

IT was another market day at Gbedun, the little village where I worked at the local government health center. Being a community of farmers, the villagers had all gone to sell their crops at the weekly market, and attendance at the clinic was therefore very poor. Having spent the last few weeks attending to the victims of a recent cholera epidemic in the village, I found the quiet morning a welcome change.

As I settled down in my consulting room to browse through the previous day's papers, I heard a knock on the door. In came Akpan, my theater assistant and, presumably, my best friend in the village.

"Good morning, Doctor Boye," the young man said.

"Good morning, Akpan."

"I'm sorry about last night, Doctor," Akpan said, still bleary eyed from our late outing the previous night.

"Forget it, Akpan. It was nothing," I said as my mind recalled the previous night.

It's amazing how an ordinary game of Draught could make two

friends quarrel. I had engaged Akpan in one of our regular games after the evening ward round. Everything went on well until the fifth game when I turned round to slap a mosquito at the nape of my neck. Suddenly, I thought I saw a movement from Akpan. My suspicion was confirmed when he made the next move and quickly captured four of my pieces in a row.

"Ha, Akpan, how can that be? You must have shifted the pieces while I was not looking," I had protested.

"True to God, Doctor, I never did that," the chap had countered.

But I was sure that he had cheated and I told him so. He insisted on his innocence and before long an argument had ensued. We broke up minutes later, swearing at each other.

Now he was here, standing in front of me, with a mischievious grin plastered on his face.

"We have a patient, Doctor," he announced.

"Another emergency?" I asked.

"Something like that, Doctor. He's my landlord."

"Where is he?" I asked, becoming a bit suspicious. Though I could tolerate Akpan's posing to the villagers as a doctor, I found it difficult to condone his occasional practice of treating patients in his one-room apartment located somewhere in the village. In fact, rumors had it that the chap made a lot of money from this nefarious practice.

Akpan quickly brought in an elderly man who had a piece of bloodstained rag covering his mouth.

"What's wrong with him?" I asked.

"It's one of his teeth, Doctor," Akpan volunteered, suddenly finding it difficult to meet my eyes. "The tooth was rotten and shaking so he said he wanted it out. So I—I—" He hesitated and stopped.

"Go on, Akpan. So you removed it?"

"I tried to remove it, Doctor," Akpan said, shifting from one foot to the other.

"In your *clinic*?" I asked.

"No, Doctor. I don't have any clinic," the lad said smiling. "I tried it in the dressing room."

"When did we start pulling teeth in this place?" I asked in annoyance.

"I'm sorry, Doctor, but Dr. Ali used to do it so—"

"That was Dr. Ali. I refer cases like this to the dentist in Shagamu. At any rate, since you've started, let's see what's there," I said as I directed the patient to sit. I looked in his mouth but a pool of blood and saliva obscured my view. "Rinse your mouth and spit into the basin," I directed.

I was soon able to see the rotten tooth still held by one of its roots, from where blood was ozzing at an alarming rate.

"He won't make it to Shagamu," I said.

"It's almost out," Akpan added, peering from behind me. "All it needs is a little tug," he added.

I debated the issue for a while in my mind. Much as I disliked dabbling into such cases, the old man might lose a lot of blood before reaching Shagamu, which is about a hundred kilometers away.

"Okay, where are the instruments?" I asked moments later as I rolled up my sleeves.

Akpan produced one old pair of pliers.

"You mean this is all we have?"

"Yes, Doctor. That's What Dr. Ali normally used!"

"What of the Xylocaine?" I asked referring to the local anaesthetic.

"We don't have any. We used the remaining one on that small girl yesterday," Akpan replied.

Though I suspected that the chap must have pilfered the stuff, I decided not to press him further. I merely shook my head. "I'm sorry, I can't remove the tooth without anaesthesia. Better for the man to try Shagamu than dying on my hands from pain."

"I have something we can use, Doctor," Akpan now said as he groped for something in the bag he carried.

"What's that?"

"It's Ogogoro, Doctor. I bought it in Ikorodu the other day," Akpan said as he produced a bottle of locally brewed whisky.

"You mean—" I started in alarm.

"Yes, Doctor. Dr. Ali used to prescribe it. Said it's better than Xylocaine."

Akpan gave his landlord three glasses of Ogogoro, and having confirmed that the old man was drunk enough not to feel any pain, we set to work.

"Akpan, you hold back his head while I pull on the tooth. Right?"

"Right, Doctor," Akpan replied as he squatted to get a good grip on the elderly man's head.

I grabbed the offending tooth with the pliers and pulled with all my strength but the tooth remained firm.

"Try putting your right knee on his chest, Doctor," Akpan advised.

I winced. Even with that, we didn't make much progress and before long I started panting.

"Let me go for Hassan," Akpan said, referring to the ambulance driver.

Hassan soon appeared and Akpan promptly took over control. "Give me the pliers, Doctor. Hassan, you hold back the head while I pull. Doctor, you pull me by the abdomen," Akpan said as he now grabbed the rotten tooth with the pliers. "All right, Doctor? As soon as I pull, you also pull."

"Okay," I grunted.

"Now! P-U-L-L!" Akpan said.

With my two hands tightly clasped around the chap's midriff, I pulled with all my might. Suddenly, the tooth came out in a flurry of saliva and blood and I went flying with Akpan on top of me, to crash at the other end of the room.

"Are you all right, Doctor?" Akpan asked as he got off my stomach, the pliers and tooth still in his hand.

I nodded. And as I stood rubbing a painful bump at the back of my head Akpan said, "If I may say so, Doctor, you really know how to pull. You did it better than Dr. Ali used to do."

Born in 1955, in Nigeria, Wale Okediran is an author and medical doctor. He attended the University of Ife where he was the editor of a campus newspaper as well as an active member of the university hockey team. His poetry and short stories appear in Nigeria and other countries. His wife, Folake, is a lawyer. They are proud of their three daughters.

"One thing she was sure of amidst all the wild and agonizing speculation: her man loved her and their children..."

In Corner B

BY ES'KIA MPHAHLELE

HOW can boys just stick a knife into someone's man like that? Talita mused. Leap out of the dark and start beating up a man and then drive a knife into him. What do the parents of such boys think of them? What does it matter now? I'm sitting in this room weeping till my heart wants to burst...

Talita's man was at the government mortuary, and she sat waiting, waiting and thinking in her house. A number of stab wounds had done the job, but it wasn't till he had lain in hospital for a few hours that the system caved in and he turned his back on his people, as they say. This was a Thursday. But if one dies in the middle of the week, the customary thing is to wait for a week and be buried at the first weekend after seven days. A burial must be on a weekend to give as many people as possible an opportunity to attend it. At least a week must be allowed for the next-of-kin to come from the farthest parts of the country.

There are a number of things city folk can afford to do

precipitately: a couple may marry by special license and listen to enquiries from their next-of-kin after the fact; they can be precipitate in making children and marry after the event; children will break with their parents and lose themselves in other townships; many people do not hold coming-out parties to celebrate the last day of a newborn baby's month-long confinement in the house. But death humbles the most unconventional, the hardest rebel. The dead person cannot simply be packed off to the cemetery. You are a person because of other human beings, you are told. The aunt from a distant province will never forgive you if she arrives and finds the deceased buried before she has seen his lifeless face for the last time. Between the death and the funeral, while the body lies in the mortuary (which has to be paid for) there is a wake each night. Day and night relatives and friends and their relatives and their friends come and go, saying words of consolation to the bereaved. And all the time some next-of-kin must act as spokesman to relate the circumstances of death to all who arrive for the first time. Petty intrigues and dramatic scenes among the relatives as they prepare for the funeral are innumerable. Without them, a funeral doesn't look like one.

Talita slept where she sat, on a mattress spread out on the floor in a corner, thinking and saying little, and then only when asked questions like: "What will you eat now?" or "Has your headache stopped today?" or "Are your bowels moving properly?" or "The burial society wants your marriage certificate, where do you keep it?" Apart from this, she sat or lay down and thought.

Her man was tall, not very handsome, but lovable; an insurance agent who moved about in a car. Most others in the business walked from house to house and used buses and electric trains between townships. But her man's firm was prosperous and after his fifteen years' good service it put a new car at his disposal. Merman had soft, gentle eyes and was not at all as vivacious as she. Talita often teased him about his shyness and what she called the weariness in his tongue because he spoke little. But she always prattled on and on, hardly ever short of topics to talk about.

"Ah, you met your match last night, mother-of-Luka," her man would say, teasingly.

"My what—who?"

"The woman we met at the dance and talked as if you were not there."

"How was she my match?"

"Don't pretend to be foolish—*hau*, here's a woman! She talked you to a standstill and left you almost wide-mouthed when I rescued you. Anyone who can do that takes the flag."

"*Ag*, get away! And anyhow if I don't talk enough my tongue will rot and grow moldy."

They had lived through nineteen years of married life that yielded three children and countless bright and cloudy days. It was blissful generally, in spite of the physical and mental violence around them; the privation; police raids; political strikes and attendant clashes between the police and boycotters; death; ten years of low wages during which she experienced a long spell of ill health. But like everybody else Talita and her man stuck it through. They were in an urban township and like everybody else they made their home there. In the midst of all these living conditions, at once in spite of and because of them, the people of Corner B alternately clung together desperately and fell away from the center; like birds that scatter when the tree on which they have gathered is shaken. And yet for each individual life, a new day dawned and set, and each acted out his own drama which the others might never know of or might only get a glimpse of or guess at.

For Talita, there was that little drama which almost blackened things for herself and her man and children. But because they loved each other so intensely, the ugliest bend was well negotiated, and the cloud passed on, the sun shone again. This was when a love letter fell into her hands owing to one of those clumsy things that often happen when lovers become stupid enough to write to each other. Talita wondered about something, as she sat huddled in the corner of her dining-sitting room and looked at the flame of a candle nearby, now quivering, now swaying this way and that and now coming into an erect position as if it lived a separate life from the stick of wax. She wondered how or why it happened that a mistress should entrust a confidential letter to a stupid messenger who in turn sends someone else without telling him to return the letter if the man should be out; why the second messenger should give the letter to her youngest child who then opens it and calls his mother from the bedroom to read it. Accident? Just downright brazen cheek on the part of the mistress...!

A hymn was struck and the wake began in earnest. There was singing, praying, singing, preaching in which the deceased was mentioned several times, often in vehement praise of him and his kindness. The room filled rapidly, until the air was one thick choking lump of grief. Once during the evening someone fainted. "An aunt of the deceased, the one who loved him most," a whisper escaped from someone who seemed to know and it was relayed from mouth to mouth right out into the yard where some people stood or sat. "Shame! Shame!" one could hear the comment from active sympathizers. More than once during the evening a woman screamed at high pitch. "The sister of the deceased," a whisper escaped, and it was relayed. "Shame! Shame!" was the murmured comment. "Ao, God's people!" an old man exclaimed. During the prayers inside the people outside continued to speak in low tones.

"Have the police caught the boys?"

"No—what, when has a black corpse been important?"

"But they have been asking questions in Corner B today."

"Hm."

"When's a black corpse been important?"

"Das right, just ask him."

"It is Saturday today and if it was a white man lying there in the mortuary the newspapers would be screaming about a manhunt morning and evening since Thursday, the city would be upside down, God's truth."

"No, look here you men, these boys don't mean to kill nobody. Their empty stomachs and no work to do turns their head on evil things."

"Ag, you and your politics. Let one of them break into your house or ra—"

The speaker broke off short and wiped his mouth with his hands as if to remove pieces of a foul word hanging carelessly from his lip.

"Das not the point," squeaked someone else.

Just then the notes of a moving hymn rolled out of the room and the men left the subject hanging and joined enthusiastically in the singing, taking different parts.

Some women were serving tea and sandwiches. A middle-aged man was sitting at a table in a corner of the room. He had a notebook in front of him, in which he entered the names of those who donated money and the amounts they gave. Such collections were meant to help meet funeral expenses. In fact they went into buying tea, coffee, bread and even groceries for meals served to guests who came from far.

"Who put him there?" asked an uncle of the deceased in an anxious tone, pointing at the money collector.

"Do I know?" an aunt said.

The question was relayed in whispers in different forms. Every one of the next-of-kin denied responsibility. It was soon discovered that the collector had mounted the stool on his own initiative.

"But don't you know that he has long fingers?" the same uncle flung the question in a general direction, just as if it were a loud thought.

"I'm going to tell him to stop taking money. *Hei*, Cousin Stoffel, take that notebook at once, otherwise we shall never know what has happened to the money." Cousin Stoffel was not fast, but he had a reputation for honesty.

It was generally known that the deposed man appeared at every death house where he could easily be suspected to be related to the deceased, and invariably used his initiative to take collections and dispose of some of the revenue. But of course several of the folks who came to console Talita could be seen at other vigils and funerals by those who themselves were regular customers. The communal spirit? Largely. But also they were known to like their drinks very much. So a small fund was usually raised from the collections to buy liquor from a shebeen nearby and bring it to the wake.

Bang in the middle of a hymn a man came into the room and hissed while he made a beckoning sign to someone. Another hiss, yet another. An interested person who was meanly being left out immediately sensed conspiracy and followed those who answered the call. As they went out, they seemed to peel off a layer of the hymn and carry it out with them as they sang while moving out. In some corner of the yard or in the bedroom, a group of men, and sometimes a woman or two, conducted a familiar ritual.

"God's people," an uncle said solemnly, screwing up his face in an attempt to identify those who had been called. If he saw a stray one or two, he merely frowned but could do nothing about it on such a solemn occasion. The gatecrashers just stood, half-shy, and half-sure of themselves, now rubbing a nose, now changing postures.

"God's people, as I was about to say, here is an ox for slaughter." At this point he introduced a bottle of brandy. One did not simply plant a whole number of bottles on the floor: that was imprudent. "Cousin Felang came driving it to this house of sorrow. I have been given the honor of slaughtering it, as the uncle of this clan." With this he uncorked the bottle and served the brandy, taking care to measure with his fingers.

"This will kill the heart for a time so that it does not break from grief. Do not the English say *drown de sorry?*" He belched from deep down his stomach.

And then tongues began to wag. Anecdotes flew as freely as the drinks. And when they could not contain their mirth they laughed. "Yes, God's people," one observed, "the great death is often funny."

They did not continually take from the collections. If they felt they were still thirsty, someone went round among those he suspected felt the thirst too, and collected money from them to buy more drinks for another bout.

At midnight the people dispersed. The next-of-kin and close friends would alternate in sleeping in Talita's house. They simply huddled against the wall in the same room and covered themselves with blankets.

Talita sat and waited at her corner like a fixture in the house.

The children were staying with a relative and would come back on Sunday to see their father for the last time in his coffin. The corpse would be brought home on Saturday afternoon.

Thoughts continued to mill round in Talita's mind. A line of thought continued from where it had been cut off. One might imagine disjointed lines running around in circles. But always she wanted to keep the image of her man in front of her. Just as though it were an insult to the memory of him when the image escaped her even once.

Her man had confessed without making any scene at all. Perhaps it was due to the soft and timid manner in which Talita had asked him about the letter. She said she was sorry she had taken the letter from the child and, even when she had seen that instead of beginning "Dear Talita" it was "My everything," she had yielded to the temptation to read it. She was very sorry, she said, and added something to the effect that if she hadn't known, and he continued to carry on with the mistress, it wouldn't have been so bad. But the knowing it...Her man had promised not to see his mistress again. Not that his affair had detracted in any way from the relationship between man and wife, or made the man neglect the welfare of his family. Talita remembered how loyal he had been. The matter was regarded as closed and life had proceeded unhaltingly.

A few months later, however, she had noticed things, almost imperceptible; had heard stray words outside the house, almost inaudible or insignificant, which showed that her man was seeing his mistress. Talita had gone out of her way to track "the other woman" down. No one was going to share her man with her, fullstop, she said to herself.

She had found her: Marta, also a married woman. One evening Talita, when she was sure she could not be wrong in her suspicions, had followed Marta from the railway station to the latter's house in another part of Corner B. She entered shortly after the unsuspecting hostess. Marta's husband was in. Talita greeted both and sat down.

"I am glad you are in, *Morena*—sir. I have just come to ask you to chain your bitch. That is my man and mine alone." She stood up to leave.

"Wait, my sister," Marta's husband said. "Marta!" he called to his wife who had walked off saying laughingly and defiantly, "Aha, ooh," perhaps to suppress any feeling of embarrassment, as Talita thought. She wouldn't come out.

"You know, my sister," the man said with disturbing calm, "you know a bitch often answers to the sniffing of a male. And I think we both have to do some fastening." He gave Talita a piercing look which made her drop her eyes. She left the house. So he knows too, she thought. That look he gave her told her they shared the same apprehensions. Her man had never talked about the incident, although she was sure that Marta must have told him of it. Or would she have the courage to?

Often there were moments of deep silence as Talita and her man sat together or lay side by side. But he seldom stiffened up. He would take her into his arms and love her furiously and she would respond generously and tenderly, because she loved him and the pathos in his eyes.

"You know, my man," she ventured to say one evening in bed, "if there is anything I can help you with, if there is anything you would like to tell me, you mustn't be afraid to tell me. There may be certain things a woman can do for her man which he never suspected she could do."

"Oh, don't worry about me. There is nothing you need do for me." And, like someone who had at last found a refuge after a rough and dangerous journey, her man would fold her in his arms and love her.

Was this it, she wondered? But how? Did it begin during her long period of ill health—this Marta thing? Or did it begin with a school episode? How could she tell? Her man never talked about his former boy-girl attachments, except in an oblique or vague way which yielded not a clue. Marta was pretty, no doubt. She was robust, had a firm waist and seemed to possess in physical appearance all that could attract a man. But if she, Talita, failed to give her man something Marta had to offer, she could not trace it. How could she? Her man was not the complaining type, and she often found out things that displeased him herself and set out to put them out of his way if she could. In the morning, while he was asleep, she would stare into his broad face to see if she could read something. But all she saw was the face she loved. Funny that you saw your man's face every day almost and yet you couldn't look at it while he slept without the sensation of some guilt or something timid or tense or something held in suspension: so that if the man stirred, your heart gave a leap as you turned your face away. One thing she was sure of amidst all the wild and agonizing speculation: her man loved her and their children...

"They're always doing this to me I do not matter I cannot allow plans to be made over the body of my cousin without my being told about it and why do they talk behind my back I don't stand for dusty nonsense me. And someone's daughter has the cheek to say I am nobody in the family of my cousin and say to me, I am always going ahead of others yes I am always running ahead of the others because I think other people are fools what right has she to talk behind my back why does she not tell me face to face what she thinks of me she is afraid I can make her see her mother if once I..."

"Sh!" The senior uncle of the dead man cut in to try to keep the peace. And he was firm. "What do you want to turn this house into? There is a widow in there in grief and here you are you haven't got what the English call respection. Do you want all the people around to laugh at us, think little of us? All of us bury our quarrels when we come together to weep over a dear one who has left; what nawsons is this?"

The cousin who felt outraged stood against the wall with her hands hidden behind her apron like a child caught in an act of mischief. She had not been addressing herself to anyone in particular and hoped someone would pick up the challenge. And although she felt rebuked, she said, "But uncle-of-the-clan, these people are always whispering dirty things behind my back what should I say? And then they go and order three buses instead of four these God's people have collected money for us to hire enough buses for them I shall not be surprised if someone helped himself to some of the money—"

"Sh!" the senior uncle interrupted. "We do not throw urine out of the chamber for everybody to see."

Someone whispered. *Mapodisa!* Police! With two boys! Everyone in the yard stood still, as if to some command. An African constable came in, preceded by two dirty-looking youngsters in handcuffs.

"Stop!" he barked when they neared the door.

"Where is the widow?" the constable asked, addressing no one in particular.

Silence.

"*Hela!* Are these people dumb?" Silence. One of the boys blew his nose on to the ground with his free hand and wiped off the stuff from his upper lip and ran the hand down the flank of his trousers.

The constable went into the room with a firm stride, almost lifting the boys clear of the ground in the process. Inside, he came face to face with Talita, who was sitting in her usual corner. She seemed to look through him, and this unsettled him slightly. He braced himself up visibly.

"Face the mother there you fakabond!" he barked at the boys.

"I say look at the mother there, you dirty *tsotsi.*" He angrily lifted the drooping head of one of them.

"You know this mother?" The boys shook their heads and mumbled.

"Mother, look at these *tsotsis.* Have you ever seen them before? Look at them carefully, take your time."

Talita looked at them wearily. She shook her head.

"Sure-sure?" Again she shook her head.

"I know what you do at night, you fakabond." The whole house was now full of him, the rustle of his khaki uniform and his voice and his official importance. "You kill, you steal, you rape and give other people no peace. Fakabond! You saw boys attack a man the other night, did you? Dung, let me tell you! You talk dung. Pure dung! You took out your knives for the man, fakabond! You see that bucket in front of your cells? You will fill it in quick time tonight when the *baas* is finished with you. This big white sergeant doesn't play around with black boys like you as I do. Dung! You didn't mean to kill him, you say, just wanted to beat him up and he fought back. Dung!"

The constable had hardly said the last word when an elderly woman came out of another room, holding a stick for support.

"What is all this?" she asked. "First you come and shake this poor child out of her peace when she has lost her man and then you use foul words at a time like this. Cannot this business wait until after the burial? Tell me who are you? Who is your father? Where were you born?"

He mumbled a few words, but the woman cut him short.

"Is this how you would like your mother or your wife to be treated, I mean your own own mother?"

"I am doing the government's work."

"Go and tell that government of yours that he is full of dung to send you to do such things. *Seis! Kgoboromente, kgoboromente!* You and him can go to hell where you belong. Get out!"

She took a lunge and landed her stick on him. Once, then twice, and the third time she missed because the constable dashed noisily out of the house, hauling the boys by the handcuffs. The woman pursued him with a limp, right up to the car in which was a white man in plain clothes—directly in front of the gate. The white man was obviously at pains to suppress a laugh. The constable entered with the boys in a most disorderly, undignified manner...The vehicle started off amidst the clatter of words that continued to come from the woman's mouth.

Talita wondered: were the boys merely the arms of some monster sitting in the dark somewhere, wreaking vengeance on her man...?

Evening came. One caucus after another was held to make sure all arrangements were intact; for this was Saturday and the corpse had arrived. The double-decker buses from the city transport garages: were they booked? You son of Kobe did you get the death certificate and permit for the cemetery? And the number plate? They want to see the dead man's pass first. Ask for it in the house...Pass pass be damned, cannot a man go to his grave in peace without dragging his chains after him...! Is the pastor coming tonight? Those three goats: have they been slaughtered? Right, this is how men work...You have worked well. The caucus meetings went on...

Word went round that the grandmother of the deceased had come. She loved Talita, so everyone who mattered testified. Heads nodded. Relatives who had not seen one another for a long time were there and family bonds were in place again. Some who were enemies tolerated each other, shooting side-glances at each other. Those who loved each other tended to exaggerate and exhibit the fact.

The people came in to keep vigil for the last night. The brown coffin—not ostentatious enough to cause a ripple of tell-tale excitement—stood against a wall. A white sheet was thrown across to partition the room so that in the smaller portion the corpse lay on a mattress under a white sheet. Talita sat next to it, leaning against her man's grandmother. The days and nights of waiting had told on her face; the black head-tie that was fastened like a hood cast a shade over it. Her hair had already been reduced to look like a schoolgirl's with a pair of scissors. Singing began. The elderly ladies washed the corpse. The tune sailed out of the room, floated in the air and was caught by those outside.

"Tomorrow after the funeral, eh? O.K.?"

"Yes, tomorrow after the funeral. Where?"

"At the party."

"Oh-*ja*. I forgot Cy's party. I'll go home first and change, eh? But I'm scared of my Pa."

"Let the old beard go fly a kite."

"He's my pa all the same." She pushed him slightly as a reproach.

"O.K. He is, so let's not fight 'bout it. Still, don't you want me to come to your house?"

"You know he don't like you and he'd kill me if he saw me with you."

"Because you work and I don't, I'm sure. I'm getting a job Monday: that'll fix the old beard."

"No, it's not just a job and it's not you Pa hates."

"That's funny talk. What then?"

"Just because I'm twenty-three and I shouldn't have a boy yet."

"Jesus! Where's the old man been living all these years? Jesus!"

"Doesn't matter, Bee. You're my boy." She giggled.

"What's funny?"

"Just remembered my pa asked me the other day who's that he saw me with. I say your name—Bee, I say."

"And then?"

"And then his face becomes sour and he says Who? I say Bee. He says Where have you heard someone called Bee—*Bee* did you say? I say anybody can call his son what he likes. He says you must be mad or a *tsotsi* without even a decent name."

A deep sigh and then: "That's not funny." He trembled slightly.

"Don't be cross Bee, you know it means nothing to me what you're called."

"Sh—they're praying now."

Two mouths and two tongues suck each other as he presses her against the wall of the shed that served as a fowl-run.

"Hm, they're praying," but her words are lost in the other's mouth. He feels her all over and she wriggles against him. She allows herself to be floored...

A hymn strikes again.

Two figures heave themselves up from the ground, panting. It has been a dark, delicious, fugitive time. They go back and join the singers, almost unnoticed.

The hymn continues. A hymn of hope, of release by death, of refuge for the weary and tormented: a surrender to death once it has been let loose among a flock of sheep. Underlying the poetry of this surrender is the one long and huge irony of endurance.

In another corner of the yard an elderly man was uncorking a bottle of whisky and pouring it into glasses. The sound of it, like water flowing down a rock crevice, was pleasing to the ear as the company squatted in front of the *priest*. Here my children, kill the heart and as the Englishman says, *drown de sorry*. Ah, you see now...Someone, for lack of something important or relevant to say, but out of sheer blissful expectation, sighed: "*Ja Madoda*—yes, men, death is a strange thing. If he came to my house he would ask my woman to give him food any time and he could come any time of night and say I've come to see if you're all right and then we would talk and talk and talk. We were so close. And now he's late, just like that." And he sobbed and sniffled.

"*Ja*," the others sighed in chorus.

A woman screamed in the room and broke into sobs. The others carried her out.

"Quiet child," a middle-aged woman coaxed. "Quiet, quiet, quiet." Talita held out. When Sunday dawned she said in her heart God let it pass this time. The final act came and passed...

They were all walking away from the grave towards the tarmac path leading to the exit. Suddenly a woman, seemingly from nowhere, went and flung herself on the soft, red, damp mound of the new grave. It was Marta. She screamed like one calling a person across a river in a flood, knowing the futility of it all. "Why did you leave me alone?" Marta yelled, her arms thrown over her head. Her legs kicked as she cried unashamedly, like a child whose toy has been wrenched out of his hand. Soon there was one long horizontal gasp as whispered words escaped the crowd, underlining the grotesqueness of the scene. Some stood stolidly, others amused, others outraged.

Two men went and dragged Marta away, while she still cried, "Come back, come back, why did you leave me alone?"

Talita stopped short. She wanted badly to leap clear of the hands that supported her, but she was too weak. The urge strained every nerve, every muscle of her body. The women who supported her whispered to her to ignore the female's theatrics. "Let us go, child," they said. "She wants you to talk." They propelled Talita towards the black "family car."

A few days later, a letter arrived, addressed to Talita. She was walking about in the yard, but was not allowed to go to work or anywhere beyond the gate. The letter was in a bad but legible scrawl and read:

"Dear Missis Molamo, I am dropping this few lines for to hoping that you are living good now i want to telling you my hart is sore sore. i hold myselfe bad on the day of you're mans funeral my hart was ful of pane too much and i see myselfe already o Missis Molamo alreaddy doing mad doings i think the gods are beatting me now for holding myselfe as wyle animall forgeef forgeef i pray with all my hart child of the people."

Talita paused. These wild women who can't even write must needs try to do so in English. She felt the tide of anger and hatred mounting up, flushing her whole body, and then she wondered if she should continue to read. She planted her elbow on the table and supported her head with her hand. She felt drawn to the letter, so she obeyed the impulse to continue.

"now i must tel you something you must noe quik quik thees that i can see that when you come to my hause and then whenn you see me kriing neer the grafe i can see you think i am sweet chokolet of your man i can see you think in your hart my man love that wooman no no i want to tel you that he neva love me nevaneva he livd same haus my femily rented in Fitas and i lovd him mad i tel you i lovd him mad i wanted him with red eyes he was nise leetl bit nise to me but i see he sham for me as i have got no big ejucashin he got too much book i make nise tea and cake fo him and he like my muther and he is so nise i want to foss him to love me but he just nise i am shoor he come to meet me in toun now we are 2 marryd peeople bicos he remember me and muther looked aftar him like bruther for me he was stil nise to me but al wooman can see whenn there is no loveness in a man and they can see lovfulness. now he is gonn i feel i want to rite with my al ten fingas becos i have too muche to say aboute your sorriness and my sorriness i will help you to kry you help me to kry and leev that man in peas with his gods. so i stop press here my deer i beg to pen off the gods look after us

i remain your sinserity
Missis Marta Shuping."

When Talita finished reading, a great dawn was breaking upon her, and she stood up and made tea for herself. She felt like a foot traveler after a good refreshing bath.

Born in Pretoria, Es'kia Mphahlele, a remarkable man of letters, attended elementary school locally and high school in Johannesburg. He studied for his B.A. degree by correspondence with the University of South Africa and was granted the degree in 1949. In 1956 he was awarded his M.A. degree in English literature and in 1968 was awarded a Ph.D. from the University of Denver, in the USA. He taught in South Africa until 1952 when he was banned from teaching by the Government as a result of campaigning against against "Bantu Education" as general secretary of the Teachers Association. During his years of exile he traveled widely in Africa, Europe and the USA, and taught at various universities. He returned to South Africa in 1977 despite being "listed" under the Internal Security Act, which was lifted in 1979. His work includes short stories, plays, novels and essays. In addition to his mother tongue, Es'kiel Mphahlele speaks French, English, Dutch, Spanish and Zulu.

"Pascual Cano thought that it would have been too much to expect, just for once, that something would work out as he wished."

Overbooking

BY ANDRÉS FORNELLS

ON that particular day, Pascual Cano, the head receptionist of the Sargazo Hotel, considered himself the most problem-affected man in the whole world. His wife would at any moment give birth, his father was hanging between life and death, his oldest son had a knee tumor and he himself had to deal with very serious overbookings.

Overwrought, Pascual Cano spent the morning calling different hotels—some of them very expensive—but he was unable to find accommodations for his surplus clients in any of them.

Full of anguish, he smoked one cigarette after another, thinking that with his bad luck surely lung cancer was already spreading within him. He studied the day's reservations once again and picked out the definite "victims" of the overbookings: the Culby family—one double and triple room, Mrs. Langefield, Mr. Swanson, Miss Brough and Mr. Tommas—all for single rooms. The Culby family would all have to room together—in single beds—in the television room; Mrs. Langefield and Mr. Swanson could be put into a single room with two beds and, with some luck, there might still be a screen around to put between the beds. They were both over sixty-five years old and probably very particular about their privacy; Miss Brough—twenty-four—and Mr. Tommas—twenty-seven. Perhaps they would be willing to share a single room with two beds. Experience had proven to Pascual Cano that to many young people this kind of arrangement was so well appreciated that it often could last until the end of the holiday, and it was not unusual that those couples thrown together eventually ended up marrying, as letters of gratitude later showed.

At a quarter past one, the first bus packed with smiling and excited tourists arrived. The head receptionist, with a face the length of a wet week, requested passports and signatures and distributed keys. He asked the Culby family and the other chosen few, to stay behind for a moment. All of them seemed a little surprised, but no one protested.

Then Pascual Cano went into his small office, seated himself at his desk which was covered by an authentic mountain of papers, and said to his assistant:

"Show the Culbys in, please, Miguel."

"Good luck, Chief," the young receptionist whispered, giving Pascual Cano a very compassionate look.

The Culby parents were both short and stout. Their faces mirrored ingenuousness. The head receptionist noted their calloused hands and surmised they were farmers, or something along that line. This cheered him a bit, but not very much because no rule can be expected to be infallible. But, normally, country people are much easier to handle than townfolk.

Following his kind invitation, the Culbys seated themselves in front of him. They seemed rather nervous.

Pascual Cano, in deep consternation, told them one of his best stories:

"I'm so upset, so terribly sorry, so desperate, that I do not know how to begin...Just yesterday, a very unfortunate fire destroyed the two rooms destined for you and your children. And it will take, at the very least, a few days to restore and paint them. Since that disastrous accident I have called on all the hotels on the coast, even the most luxurious ones, pleading room for you. But as it is high season, they have been unable to give me even a single room. So, the only possibility is to offer you the television room for tonight—tremendously big—and tomorrow, probably, a room in the hotel. Of course, we will compensate you for the inconvenience by giving a nice discount off the total amount you have paid your agency. Please, Mrs. and Mr. Culby, help me with your understanding! I'm so unhappy I could die!"

The head receptionist, his face reflecting his tremendous desperation, was on the verge of tears.

The Culbys exchanged a look of total disconcertion. Mrs. Culby was the first to react.

"But we will need some place to change our clothes during the day," she ventured almost apologetically.

The woman's resigned attitude produced a great sense of relief in the depressed Pascual Cano.

"No problem, madam," he said, sweet as honey. "First, all of you go and eat. When you have finished, your baggage will be brought here, to my office, which you can use as yours."

Extremely amiable, the marvelous Culbys even thanked the head receptionist.

"Very obliged to you, sir," they said.

"It's I who is obliged to you. You are wonderful people. Thank you very much!"

The head receptionist's words were completly sincere. He accompanied the Culbys to the door.

All did not go smoothly with Mrs. Langefield and Mr. Swanson. Both were intransigent and disagreeable, taking the proposition of sharing the same room as intolerable abuse and demanding the presence of their courier, Susan York, the representative of the More Sunshine agency.

Susan York, who knew that to survive in the competition of prices, the hotels were forced to overbook during the high season, listened attentively to the complaints of the two older clients. Then she quietly explained that it was impossible for her to find rooms for them in other hotels, as all of them were in similar positions to the Sargazo.

"I want to return home. My holiday has been cruelly spoiled," the angry Mrs. Langefield said.

"And I don't wish to remain either," Mr. Swanson added.

Without losing her admirable calm, the courier responded, "That's impossible. There are no seats available for the next two months, on any airplane.

Blind with fury, the two tourists assured that they would bring charges against the hotel and the agency when they got back home.

As they stomped out, Pascual Cano and Susan York exchanged glances of sympathy and resignation.

"Dear Susan, when we die, we can expect only the best," Pascual said. "We have already passed through hell on earth."

"You can say that again, dear Pascual," replied the English courier. "I hope it will be better with the next couple."

"Probably they will be extremely content with the arrangement, they are both young."

"Well, in any case, I'll be in the bar if you need me."

"Thanks a million."

Miss Brough was a splendid-looking girl, with a voluptuous figure. Fully aware of her attraction to men, she flashed a smile that could melt stones. For an instant, Pascual Cano forgot his problems and deeply envied the tall, neat and handsome Mr. Tommas his good luck. Then he told them of unhappy circumstances forcing him to lodge them in a single room with a double bed, for the length of only two days. And he concluded, rather maliciously:

"Then, if you still desire it, I will be able to accommodate you in two singles."

Miss Brough showed her dazzling smile to Mr. Tommas and shrugged her shoulders, clearly pleased.

"It is all right with me," she said softly, her voice pure sugar.

Incomprehensibly, Mr. Tommas, who had obviously paled, said, "I fully apreciate your difficulties, sir, but would it not be possible to have at least two beds?"

Very surprised at the turn of events, Pascual pleaded for patience until the following day when he could grant Mr. Tommas his wish. Pascual could not understand the man's reluctance to share a bed with the magnificent and well predisposed Miss Brough. Mr. Tommas did not look *strange*.

Finally both clients left the office, Miss Brough swinging her hips provocatively, and Mr. Tommas looking as if he just had been sentenced to death and was on his way to the scaffold.

Alone at last, the head receptionist buried his head in his hands. He was nearing the end of his tether. He rested a few moments. Then, with an unhappy sigh, he reached for the telephone and dialed his home number. His mother-in-law answered.

"Listen, Erminia. It's me. How is Alicia?" he asked with false amiability.

"Still alive. Your damn hotel is more important than your family. But some day you will see..."

Pascual hadn't the strength to enter into a discussion.

"Well, well, you know better, Erminia. And Ramoncin?"

"In bed, reading. God helps us! You don't seem in a hurry to have him operated on. You wait, wait until his leg will have to be cut off!"

"Don't say that again! You like only to torture me! You know we are waiting for Dr. Salgado's call. I want him to perform the surgery on Ramoncin. I have all my trust in him."

"We'll see if we do not have to cry tears of blood one of these days. You are so easy going. Have you heard anything new about your poor father?"

"No. I'm going to ring the hospital now. I hadn't time before, as I'm so busy."

"Excuses! All excuses! How unconcerned and unfeeling you are, Pascual. You should be ashamed of yourself!"

The head receptionist was too tired and sad to take offense.

"Emilia, when Alicia's labor begins, call Cousin Pedro immediately. He will drive her to the hospital. I've arranged it with him."

"Very typical of you. Yes, very. As always, here you are slipping out of your most sacred obligations. What bad luck befell my daughter the day she married you!"

The maligned son-in-law violently replaced the phone. He could not endure listening to his wife's mother any longer. After a short pause to light a cigarette, he dialed the Santa Cruz Hospital.

"Your father's condition is unchanged," Dr. Prieto informed him. "We are doing all we can for him, but don't raise your hopes too high. To be blunt, Pascual, only a miracle can save him."

"Thank you, Juan, for being honest with me. Please call me at the hotel if there is anything new."

Pascual Cano replaced the receiver. Tears gathered in his very tired eyes. His father, the person who had always truly understood him, was almost no more. Life seemed so bitter and senseless. For what was he killing himself with worries?

Quietly his assistant opened the door and asked, "Did you go to eat, Boss?"

"Oh, I don't feel hungry, Carlos."

"Try and make an effort," urged the young receptionist. "You are as thin as a piece of spaghetti. If you continue on like this, you won't see the season to an end, Boss."

"Maybe that would be the best for me," Pascual replied gloomily. "All right, tell the bellboy to bring some fruit."

Early the next morning, as Pascual walked into the Sargazo Hotel, he saw a man sleeping on the sofa at the far end of the hall.

"Who is he?" he asked the night porter.

"He said his room was 113, but he couldn't sleep in it. I asked why and he replied that he wanted to speak to you. As it was about 1 a.m. I did not want to disturb you. So I told him you have no telephone and that it was impossible to contact you."

"Well done, Agustin."

The rosy-cheeked night porter smiled, pleased with his own work.

"Shall I wake him, Mr. Cano?"

The always exhausted head receptionist promptly replied, "No, Agustin! Leave him be. And please, send a bellboy to the bar for a strong coffee for me. By the way, how is the family in the television room?"

"Oh, they are fine. Even the children. A little while ago I went to see, and all were sleeping soundly. One could say they feel happy over there, Mr. Cano."

"Great."

The head receptionist entered his small office and practically collapsed into his chair. He hardly had closed his eyes all night. Part of the time he had spent with his dying father and part in the hospital where his wife gave birth to another baby boy, their fifth. Since the birth of their second son, they had been hoping for a girl. Pascual Cano thought that it would have been too much to expect, just for once, that something would work out as he wished.

He lit another cigarette. He had smoked so many in the last anguished hours that his throat ached, but to die of lung cancer no longer worried him unduly. Death had begun to appear as a liberator.

His sad eyes traveled to the open luggage and disorderly clothes of the Culby family. With more problems of overbooking to follow that day, Pascual Cano decided to leave the Culby family in the television room a few more days. They seemed quite happy there, anyway. It was a terrible, a very unjust, thing to do but in this unfair world it is only possible to abuse good people.

The bellboy came with a steaming coffee, and some news.

"Mr. Agustin says that the man on the sofa wants to speak with you now, Mr. Cano."

"Oh God," sighed Pascual, "I can't even drink my coffee in peace. All right. Show him in."

The bellboy left and within seconds Mr. Tommas entered. The sad and irritated eyes of Pascual Cano opened to the point of falling out. Mr. Tommas wore a dark suit and the white collar of a priest! Now the man's reluctance to share a bed with the sensual Miss Brough was very clear.

One more sin to add to my enormous collection. Sacrilege! thought the surprised Pascual.

"Please, sir," pleaded the priest, joining his hands as in prayer, "give me another room. That woman, Miss Brough, is the devil himself! She tried to seduce me the very moment we went to bed. To stop her, I told her that I am a priest. But this served only to excite her even more. She told me she was dying with desire to have one of my sort. Never in my entire life has God placed me in such an extreme position. That dreadful, sinful woman awakened temptations that I had surpressed to the deepest regions of my being. God be blessed that I got the will to escape from her at the very last moment. Never before has my soul been at greater risk."

Pascual Cano slowly shook his head, prematurely graying at the temples. His coffee had already turned cold. He was at the point of suggesting to Mr. Tommas that he continue sleeping on the sofa for a few more nights until he got the single room he was entitled to, when the phone rang.

It was Dr. Prieto giving him the bad news that his poor father had passed away without recovering consciousness or suffering any pain. The doctor extended his sympathy.

The pain inside Pascual became acute although he had been expecting this news. Dr. Prieto continued speaking, telling Pascual of the plans for the disposal of the deceased's body. He said it would remain in the hospital until the time of the funeral.

Heartsore, Pascual Cano replaced the receiver, drank his cold coffee and, finally looking at Mr. Tommas, Pascual said with a trembling voice and tears swimming in his eyes, "Well, Mr. Tommas, your problem is solved. You can come tonight to sleep at my house. One of the bedrooms has suddenly been left empty."

Born in Tarrasa, Barcelona, Andrés Fornells Fayos studied law for two years before his passion for travel overcame him. He has traveled extensively, staying long enough in several countries to learn to speak well in English, German, French and Italian. His second passion, dating from his adolescence, is writing. For the last ten years, he has been writing short stories and novels influenced by his traveling experiences.

"Certainly things must be done properly, through the correct channels."

The Award

BY JANE ELSDON

IT is spring 1961. You're walking down the street and you glimpse your reflection in a store window. You shudder and something dives inside you. The reflection belongs to a stranger and not an attractive one. Too much weight has accrued in 45 years and the hair you used to brush into thick brown waves is short and parted in the middle like those pictures kids laugh at in their mothers' college yearbooks. Brown eyes, once soft as pansies, are glazed and cold.

But you haven't time to think of it now because you're late for the select dinner you're to hostess. And your husband has given the word that you are by no means to be late. He's a minister of a large, prestigious church. He and some of the "pillars" are having the dinner to interview a young man and his wife. They're considering adding him to the staff and they want to see if his wife will fit in, too.

They've chosen the fanciest restaurant in town for it. After all, he's a "Princeton man" and your husband wants to impress him. It occurs to you that you can't remember when he's wanted to impress you. And as for you—you don't feel like you could impress anybody—dumpy and dowdy in your navy blue suit. The hot July evening drenches you with humidity and you feel like Daniel going into the lion's den.

The restaurant is cool and elegant. In this plush chartruese upholstered setting, sleek and modern, you feel big and old and out of place. You see the group, and your husband spots you and dashes in your direction, hands outstretched in his most gracious public greeting.

"Ahhhh, my good wife has arrived," he gushes, taking you by the hand, leading you over to a young couple in the corner, surrounded by church officers. He is tall and ministerial looking. Just right. But you don't know about her. She's on the tallish side, too, but she doesn't look quite like a minister's wife.

You can't put your finger on it because her beige dress is plain to the point of severity, but a tiny pale green pillbox hat completely covered with silk petals and a wisp of veil sits atop her hair and matching gloves give her a chic that bothers you. Something you haven't even time to think of with dozens of speaking engagements, circle meetings, Bible classes, women's association meetings, choir rehearsals, prayer groups, board meetings and on *ad infinitum*.

Everyone likes the couple. Indeed, they fawn over them, so nicely will they fit into the country club congregation. You know before you sit down to dinner that they've been accepted already, and such easy acceptance hurts. You haven't forgotten that you, too, were accepted in the beginning. All you can think of is the limited, superficial acceptance that holds you up to the community now like Sunday morning mascots. Somehow you feel acceptance must be earned. Or at least you are still trying to earn it.

You sit beside her and talk. Something about her makes you feel you're looking into a distorting mirror. There she is—twenty-five and fresh and lovely—and you keep seeing that stranger's short, heavy, navy blue reflection. And there's this disconcerting feeling you've lost yourself somewhere along the way and it isn't really you sitting there talking to her at all. You invite her to a women's association board meeting and she agrees to come.

Your husband takes the couple to the church to show them around and you go home alone. The streets are dark and hollow, like you feel inside. The scent of orange blossoms you once inhaled eagerly with joy are a mockery in the air. Involuntarily, it summons the sting of long suppressed tears.

The day of the board meeting arrives. You force yourself to attend and the young woman appears. Rising, the president introduces the need of a project to work on. Someone suggests sending old empty medicine bottles to this hospital in Africa where they're desperate for them. Everyone thinks it's a fine idea. They have lots of old empty medicine bottles.

But you remember that no project is supposed to be carried out that doesn't go through the denomination's synod structure. So you tell them they should choose one of the projects on the official mimeographed list. They don't like it and want to send the medicine bottles, because that way they could write to this doctor and have a personal contact.

You insist it really should be done the prescribed way. Then the young woman speaks quietly. She suggests that if the women really want to send the medicine bottles, perhaps they can choose a project from the list and send the bottles, too, satisfying "channels" and personal wishes, as well. It's a good idea, but you hear your voice telling them that it must be done the right way, the prescribed way. No, they can't send the medicine bottles.

On and on the women argue. For two hours they discuss sending their old empty medicine bottles to Africa, but finally, unwillingly, they decide not to. Certainly things must be done properly, through the correct channels. Then the meeting's over and you find yourself at home without remembering how you got there.

Your husband is in and you tell him about the meeting. Those medicine bottles loom over your day like the world's tallest man-made building, and he tells you you did the right thing. Somehow you get to personal matters, but he turns you off like an old recording and leaves the house.

As the weeks go by and you watch the vivacious young woman with such an enthusiasm for people and life, you get the feeling she's an embodiment of the you you've lost. You look in the mirror and you know that a bit of attention to your hair, a decent diet, some incisive personal reassessment, a balancing and broadening of your life could bring the old you back, and with her perhaps life as you'd dreamed of it. But you know if you don't do it soon, it will be too late.

You're invited to sing in the Messiah to be performed at the Community Bowl. You feel like telling them what you'd really like to sing is Rock 'n Roll. Suddenly ghosts of twenty-year-old dreams rise up to haunt you and you find yourself wanting to do mad, magic, spontaneous things—like running on the beach at night with the wind and the waves, dancing until dawn, making love with the earth beneath you and the stars overhead.

The world within you and the world without allure in a vastness inviting your exploration. All the unwritten stories and books and poetry you've been carrying within you through these years suddenly scream for expression in a flood of feeling so intense it threatens to strangle you. You try to tell your husband how you feel. His look tells you that you're insane.

But you've never felt so sane. You talk to a psychiatrist in your church and he looks at you with comprehension and compassion. He inspires you to diet and encourages you to talk about things in your life that you hate. You have your hair styled and, more important, you pause long enough to become acquainted with the you inside. And you begin to discover that she's even better than you remembered. She is a freer, wiser you.

But your growth puts an even greater chasm between you and the man you live with. Slowly you begin to see him for what he is, a pious, pompous hollow man with his feet buried in ecclesiastical concrete. He hasn't changed in all the twenty years you've been married to him.

Eventually a decision evolves. For months you ponder it. You talk it over with your counselor and you know it's the truest, most courageous thing you've ever decided. You march up the stairs to your husband's study. He gives you that what-now look and you tell him you want to talk to him. "Well, really," he says, "I'm quite busy."

"This can't wait," you say. He gives you his so-be-it look, sighs and stares in his stiff, sanctimonious way. "I've tried to talk to you, but you don't hear me," you tell him. "But now you must. I've decided to leave."

Now he knows you're insane. He doesn't take you seriously. With the preoccupied air of one who knows you don't mean it in the first place, he tries to talk you out of it.

"I mean it," you say and something in your tone reveals you do. He's stunned for a moment. He tries to point out your foolishness, but he doesn't daunt you. Finally, you convince him you're indeed serious. He looks at you for a long moment and then says the first really honest utterance you can remember in many years: "But what will they think? What will people think? What will they say? They'll think I've failed."

Not have I failed you? Or how have I failed you? Or why have we failed each other? Or we must try—or I still care for you. But, "What will people think? What will people say?" And for the first time in twenty years you know you're free, because you don't care anymore what people think or what people say. You will live your life moment by moment guided by your own integrity and what you feel, not what others think you should feel.

Once your decision is made, you waste no time preparing to go. You gather together the things that mean a great deal to you. You're amazed and appalled at how few things from your twenty years really matter to you in your going—a few books here, some records there, a picture. You put your suitcases on the bed and empty the contents of drawers into them, one by one. When you're almost finished the doorbell interrupts you. You're breathless with your leaving, and you rush to the door.

Three women stand on the porch. They are members of your church. Attempting to stifle impatience, you invite them in. They comment on the weather and you wait for them to state their business. The small talk dribbles on and your impatience becomes a frown on your face. They're taken aback. Are they keeping you, they ask. "As a matter of fact, yes," you tell them in a burst of bravery. They look at you as if you're an insect and apologize profusely.

"We are here, Mrs. Ruhl, with lovely news. Wonderful news. Actually, just marvelous news. It's an honor. Such a great honor. We're so proud. I mean, we are simply delighted to tell you."

"Yes, yes. Go on," you prod.

"We are here to tell you that you have just been selected Minister's Wife of the Year. We all, the whole community, we agree you are absolutely the most remarkable, just the most remarkable minister's wife we've ever seen."

And you are. You most certainly are.

 *Jane Elsdon, Area Coordinator of California Poets in the Schools for San Luis Obispo County and poet-in-residence for San Luis Coastal Unified School District, teaches the writing of poetry to students from Kindergarten through high school. Over 200 of her stories, poems and non-fiction pieces have been published in magazines and newspapers, although she began writing for publication when in her forties. She writes for both children and adults.*

"That's what you were going to tell me?"

American Beauty

BY ETHAN CANIN

WHEN my brother Lawrence left us to live in California I should
have tried to stop him, but I didn't, and I should have been sad,
but I wasn't. Instead it was just something happening in our lives.
It was like the roof leaking or the electricity going out. I
thought of him riding the Trailways bus across the western states,
underneath the bubble skylight, sharing cigarettes in station diners,
talking with girls he didn't know. I thought of his new life in the
Electronics Belt. I imagined going out to see him in a couple of
years, heading out to California to stay with him in a split-level
ranch with a dark-bottom pool. He was twenty-seven and I was
sixteen and computers were booming.

On the morning he left, my mother gave him a Bible. I gave
him a watch with a built-in compass, and our sister, Darienne,
who was nineteen, gave him a four-by-six-foot oil portrait of our
family, framed.

"I'm going to have to take it out of the frame," Lawrence said.

"But it's of our family."

"Dary, I'm taking a bus." Lawrence looked at me.

"Dary," I said, "he'll break down the frame and roll up the canvas. It's done all the time."

"I worked six weeks on it," she said. She started to cry.

"Don't worry," I said. "He'll be back soon."

Lawrence held up the painting. In it we were sitting together in our kitchen—my brother, my sister, my mother, our spaniel named Caramel, and I. Lawrence's wrist dipped below the back of Darienne's collarbone so that his bad hand was hidden around her shoulder.

My father was in the painting also, or at least Darienne's idea of him. He had left fourteen years ago, and not even Lawrence remembered much about him. We certainly never talked about him anymore. But Darienne still put him into her paintings. In them he had a hooked nose, a straight nose, the faintly Indian nose and angled cheekbones that I think he really did have; he had thinning hair, full hair; he stared out from the canvases, scowled out, held his head turned away from us. He had been a civil engineer. He had stolen some money from his company and left with a woman who was one of my mother's good friends. One of the few times my mother spoke of him after that, years later, she told me that he was looking for something he would never find. In the painting Darienne now gave Lawrence he stood behind my mother. His arm rested on Darienne's shoulder, and he was smiling. He almost never smiled in Darienne's paintings.

"He's smiling," I said.

"He knows Lawrence is going to stay."

"I'm not staying, Dary."

"He's not staying," I said.

"He knows he's coming back soon, then," she said.

Lawrence was leaving because things had reached a point for him here. Although my mother said the good Lord subtracted five years from his age, the five years he spent fighting in blacktop lots and driving a car with no hood over the engine, twenty-seven was still old for him to be living where he was, in the basement of our house. He had an engineering degree from Hill Oak College and a night certificate in computer programming. His job, teaching math and auto mechanics at the high school, had ended in June, and on top of that my sister was having a bad summer. In July she had shown me a little black capsule inside the case where she kept her oboe reeds. We were alone in her room.

"Do you know what it is?"

"Cold medicine," I answered.

"Nope," she said. She put it on her tongue and closed her mouth. "It's cyanide."

"No, it's not."

"It is so."

"Dary, take that out of your mouth." I put my hand on her jaw, tried to get my finger between her lips.

"I'm not Caramel."

"Caramel wouldn't eat cyanide." I could feel the tips of her incisors nibbling my fingers. Finally I got my hand into her mouth.

"It's not cyanide," she said. "And get your hands out of my mouth." I pulled the pill out and held it on my palm. Saliva was on my fingers.

"You're crazy," I said to her. Then I regretted it. I wasn't supposed to say that to her. My mother had taken me aside a few years before and told me that even though my sister and I had lived together all our lives, I might still never understand her. "It's difficult for her to be around all you men," my mother said to me. "You and Lawrence are together somehow, and that's a lot for your sister." Then she told me never to call Darienne crazy. She said this was important, something I should never forget. I was thirteen or fourteen years old. "Whatever you do," she said, tilting her head forward and looking into my eyes, "whatever happens, I want you to remember that."

At the beginning of the summer, before I knew he was leaving, Lawrence said he had something very important to tell me. "But I'm not just going to tell you," he said. "I'll mix it into the conversation. I'll say it some time over the summer. We were working on my motorcycle, which he had given me. "You have to figure out what it is," he said. He had drilled the rusted bolts on the cam covers and we were pulling them out. "It's about time you started doing that anyway."

"Doing what?"

"Thinking about what's important."

We were living in Point Bluff, Iowa, in the two-story, back-porched saltbox my father had bought before he left us. As we took apart the rusting cams I tried to decide what was important in our lives. Nothing had changed since I could remember. Lawrence still lived in the basement, where at night the green light of his computer filled the window. Darienne was using the summer to paint still lifes and practice the Bellini oboe concerto, and I was going to go to baseball day camp in August. My mother sipped vodka cranberries out on the lawn furniture with Mrs. Silver in the evenings, and at night sat on the porch reading the newspaper or sometimes the Bible and watching the *Tonight* show. She was the high school guidance counselor and she believed the Lord had a soft spot for the dropouts and delinquents she had to talk with every day. Mrs. Silver was her best friend. Mrs. Silver was young, maybe ten years younger than my mother, and read the Bible, too, although she liked the newspaper more. My mother said she'd led a rough life. She didn't look that way to me, though. To me, my mother looked more like the one with the rough life. Sometimes she wore a bathrobe all weekend, for example. I didn't know any other mothers who did that. And except for the two or three times a week when she cooked, Lawrence and Darienne and I made our own dinners. My mother's arms were pale and her elbows were red. Mrs. Silver's were tan. Mrs. Silver wore three or four bracelets, a gold chain on her ankle, and blouses without sleeves. She came over almost every day. I talked to her sometimes in the backyard when my mother went inside to answer the phone or mix another pitcher of vodka cranberry. Mostly we talked about my future.

"It's not too early to think about college," she told me.

"I know, Mrs. Silver."

"And you ought to be saving money." She put her hands on her hips. "Are you saving money?"

"No."

"Do you know that life can be cruel?" she asked.

"Yes."

"No you don't," she said. She laughed. "You don't really know that."

"Maybe I don't."

"Are you learning, at least?"

"Yes," I answered. "I'm trying to decide what's important." I nodded. "Right now I'm learning about motorcycles."

Lawrence and I were taking apart the Honda CB 360 he had given me. We planned to have it completely rebuilt before baseball camp. He had given it to me in March, when the weather warmed and the melting snow uncovered it in the ditch by Route 80. It was green. The front fork had been bent double from impact, and when I touched the rusted chain it crumbled in my hands.

The first thing we took apart was the clutch. We loosened the striker panel and let the smooth round plates, bathed in oil, spill one by one into an aluminum turkey-roasting pan. With the oil wiped clean, they gleamed like a metal I had never seen before, the way I imagined platinum gleamed. They were polished from their own movement. Lawrence explained that the slotted panels were to dissipate heat from friction. After we took the plates out and examined them, noted how they slipped smoothly over their fellows, we put them back in. "That's how you learn a machine," he said. "You take it apart and then you put it back together."

I thought about this for a moment. "Is that what you were going to tell me?"

"No, Edgar," he said. "That's not important enough."

That spring, before he gave me the motorcycle, he had taught me his theory of machinery. In April he took me out to the back yard, to a patch of the softening earth that he had cleared of the elephant grass that grew everywhere else on the lot. He had sunk four poles there and made a shanty with fluted aluminum, sloping the ground so that snowmelt poured into two gulleys and flowed away from the center, where his machinery lay. His machinery was anything he could get his hands on. He got it from junkyards and road gulleys and farm sales. He made sealed bids on government surplus, brought home sump pumps, rifle mechanisms, an airplane engine, hauled them in a borrowed truck and set them underneath the shanty to be taken apart.

"Every machine is the same, Edgar," he told me one evening. "If you can understand two sticks hitting together, you can understand the engine of an airplane." We were standing underneath the shanty with Darienne and Mrs. Silver, who had wandered out to the backyard after dinner. Out there Lawrence kept a boulder and a block of wood and a walking stick to demonstrate the lever. "I can move the boulder with the stick," he said that evening, and then he did it. He wedged the stick between the wood and the rock, and when he leaned on it the boulder rolled over. "Fulcrum—lever—machine," he said. "Now"—and then he took the oilcloth tarp off the drag-racer engine and the Cessna propellor—" this is the very same thing."

"Spare me," said Darienne.

"If you don't want to learn," said Lawrence, "don't come out here."

Then my sister walked back across the yard, stopping to pick up a cottonweed pod for one of her still lifes. Lawrence watched her go in through the screen door. "She's crazy," he said.

I turned to him. "It's hard for her to be around all us men."

Mrs. Silver looked at me. "Good, Edgar," she said.

I smiled.

My brother picked up a wrench. He cleared his throat. "That's peckerdust," he said.

"Pardon me," said Mrs. Silver.

"I said that's peckerdust. Darienne can take what I give her. People like it when you're hard on them." He looked at her. "Everybody knows that. And you know what?" He transferred the wrench to his bad hand and pushed back his hair. "They come back for more."

"A lady wouldn't come back for more," said Mrs. Silver. She put her hands together in front of her. "And a gentleman wouldn't say that."

Lawrence laughed. "Well, Dary sure likes it. And she comes back."

"It's a nice night out here," I said.

Mrs. Silver smiled at me. "It is," she said. Then she turned and walked back to the house. The kitchen light went on. I saw Darienne at the sink putting water on her face. I watched her wipe the water from her eyes with a paper towel and then move away from the window.

Sometimes I tried to look at my sister as if she were a stranger. We spent a lot of time in the house together, she and my mother and I, and I had a lot of time to look at her. She was tall, with half-curly, half-straight hair and big shoulders. Sometimes Mrs. Silver sat with us. Mrs. Silver was lonely, my mother said. She had a husband who drank. She was beautiful, though. "I'm your mother's charity case," she would say, sitting in our yard chair while she and my mother waxed each other's legs. "Your mother just feels sorry for me." Sometimes I compared her with my sister. I watched her in the yard or on the other side of the family room as she smiled and laughed, as she brushed her bangs from her forehead or drank a vodka cranberry from a straw. Then I looked at Darienne While she painted or played oboe, as if I were seeing her for the first time at a dance, I watched her. Her hands moved. She had the potential to be pretty but she wasn't. This is what I decided. Not the way she was now, at least. Her face was friendly, but she wore boy's cotton shirts and slumped her shoulders. In her shirt pocket she kept oboe reeds, which she always sucked.

"You ought to stand up straight," Lawrence told her.

"So I can be prettier for you? I'd rather die."

"No you wouldn't," said my mother.

"And you shouldn't suck those things in public," said Lawrence.

Darienne closed her lips tight. Whenever Lawrence corrected her, she pursed them so that they turned almost white. I thought this had something to do with her epilepsy, which she'd had since childhood, but I wasn't sure. She had been a special needs student in high school. Although we were never allowed to see her report card, I think she flunked most subjects. It wasn't because she was unintelligent, my mother said to Lawrence and me, but because there was a different force driving her. She painted beautifully, for example—"like a professional," said my mother—and played second oboe in school orchestra. But something about the epilepsy, I guess, made her slow. My mother parceled out her medicine in small plastic bottles that Darienne kept on her dresser. She never had any fits—she only had the *petit mal* disease—but she slept with cloth animals in her bed at age nineteen and used a Bambi nightlight. It was small and plastic and shaped like a deer.

Although Lawrence never paid much attention to her, Darienne still liked to show him everything she made and everything she found. At the end of most days she went downstairs to the basement with sheets of her sketch paper in her hand. She stayed in his apartment for a few minutes, then came back up.

"Why do you just draw lines?" I said to her one afternoon when she came upstairs.

"I don't. I draw plenty of things."

"I've seen you just drawing lines." I grabbed her hand. "Let me see."

"Edgar, you don't care what I draw."

"I *don't* care," I said. "You're right. I just want to see."

Really, though, I did care. I wasn't sure whether I cared about her because she was my sister, or just because there was something wrong with her, but I did care. She didn't think I did, though. For my birthday that year she had given me a diary, and inside, on the flyleaf, she had written in ornate calligraphy: *I DON'T THINK YOU CARE ABOUT ANYTHING.* And below that, in small letters: (But If You Do, Write It In Here). Underneath that, she had made a sketch of the sculpture *The Thinker.* It was a good sketch, and in parentheses even lower on the page, in even smaller writing, she wrote, AUGUST RODIN.

Darienne was a good artist. In the mornings she did drawing exercises. She sat in the window bay of her bedroom, our yard and the drainage canal curving below her, the hills with their elephant grass and vanilla pines in the distance, and she drew lines. She wouldn't show me, but I saw them anyway when I was in her room. They were curved, straight, varied in thickness, drawn with the flat edge or the sharp point of the pencil.

"That's a nice one, Dary," I said one morning as I passed behind her while she was drawing at the window. "Where did you get the idea for that one?"

That afternoon she came out to the yard where Lawrence and I were pulling out tiny screws and springs from the motorcycle carburetor. "You know, Edgar," she said, "all great artists practice their lines."

"Actors practice their lines," I said.

Lawrence laughed.

She pressed her lips together. "*You* know what I mean," she said. She walked around until her shadow fell on the carburetor. Then she stood there. "Maybe now," she said, you two want to go out and shoot some animals."

"You're weird, Dary," said Lawrence.

"I'm not weird. You guys are weird." She threw a dirt clod in our oil pan. "Not everyone feels the same forces."

"You going to clean that dirt out?" said Lawrence.

"Why? So you can spend eight more hours taking out a cylinder?"

"We're working on the carburetor," I said.

"It looks like Lawrence is doing everything."

I loosened a small mixture screw. "If I practiced the oboe as much as you," I said, "I'd be Doc Severinsen."

She worked her lips. "Doc Severinsen plays the trumpet."

"He plays the oboe, too." I looked at Lawrence. I had made this up.

"The oboe is a double reed," Dary said. "It's one of the most difficult instruments."

The truth was, she was right. I had heard that the oboe was a fairly difficult instrument, and Darienne was pretty good on it. She could have played first oboe in school orchestra, but she played second because Mr. MacFarquhar, the director, didn't want her to have the responsibility. I felt bad saying the things I said to her. But she brought them on herself. I would have had conversations with her, but they never worked out.

"I hope the dirt clogs your engine," she said.

Lawrence made up a game that year that Darienne hated and that we played on all our car trips. It was called What Are You Going to Do? Lawrence drove and led the game. "You are driving along the summit pass of a mountain," Lawrence said one evening as he drove, "when under your foot you notice that the accelerator has become jammed in the full open position. You are approaching dangerous curves and the car is accelerating rapidly." He rolled down his window, propped his elbow out, adjusted the mirror to give us time to think. My mother shifted in her seat. "What are you going to do?" he asked.

"Press the brakes," said my mother.

"You'll burn them out." He adjusted his headrest.

"Steer like hell," said Mrs. Silver. Lawrence smiled.

"Open the door and roll out onto the road," said Darienne.

"You'll kill other drivers and possibly yourself." He put the blinker on and passed another car. "Edgar?"

"Shift the transmission into neutral," I answered.

"Bingo, he said. He leaned back and began whistling.

In high school, Lawrence had been in one piece of trouble after the next. He had broken windows and stolen cars and hit someone once, or so one of my teachers later told me, with a baseball bat. I knew about a lot of it because the school faculty told me. "You're Lawrence's brother," the older ones always said to me, more than a decade later, at the start of a new school year. Then they told the story about him stealing all the school's lawnmowers or driving a car into the Mississippi River. I never asked Lawrence about the bat because I couldn't imagine my brother doing that to anyone. I did ask him about some of the other things, though. He had broken into a gas station one night with his friends, poisoned a farmer's milk herd, set fifty acres of woods on fire. One night, racing, he turned too wide and drove his Chevy Malibu into the living room of a house. But he wasn't hurt. Nothing ever happened to him. He had a juvenile record and was headed, my mother said, for the other side of the green grass, when, the day he turned eighteen, like a boiling pot coming off the fire, he just stopped.

It didn't seem that anybody just changed like that, but evidently Lawrence did. This was how my mother told it. "The candle of the wicked shall be put out," she said. I was seven years old then. Lawrence was supposed to move from the house but she let him stay, and some sense just clicked on in his head. He stopped going out and his friends started calling him less, then stopped calling him completely. He cut his hair and bought a set of barbells that he lifted every evening, standing shirtless in the window of his room.

A few years later, when I was in junior high and after he had bought his computer, he began telling me to stay out of trouble. I had never gotten into any, though. I didn't want to steal cars or hit people. "It's not something I want to do," I told him.

"You will, though," he said. He looked at me. "That's for sure—you *will*. But be careful when you do." Then, to show me that he had said something serious, he put his left hand behind him. My mother had taken tranquilizers when she was pregnant with Lawrence, and now his hand had only two fingers. He always held it behind his back when he said something important. The lame fingers were wide at the knuckles and tapered at the ends, and the skin over them was shiny and waxlike. I hardly noticed it anymore. I remember my mother had once told me that Lawrence's hand was my father's legacy. She said this was how my father lived on in our lives.

I didn't understand at the time. "What do you mean?" I asked.

"It's cloven," she said.

On our family trip every June we drove for two weeks. The summer Lawrence left we started west through Nebraska and Wyoming, then south, through Utah and the Arizona desert, where we drove with wet towels hanging in the open windows. We headed west, over the Colorado River where it was wide, then back again, into canyonland, where the earth turned red and the mesas were veined with color. Darienne held a sketch pad on her knees and drew the cypress that clung to ledges in the escarpments. We turned north, into Utah, where mirages rose off the salt beds and in the distance the mountains were topped with snow. Whenever we stopped, my mother and Mrs. Silver and Darienne went on collecting trips. They came back with pieces of wood, dried seed pods, rocks with flecks of silver in them or with edges that looked polished. Darienne showed them to Lawrence.

He stood at the side of the road, smoking, one hand on the open door of the car, while she went through what they had found. A rock that looked like a face, a flower that had dried to powdery maroon. He puffed on his cigarette, looked at the things she showed him. Then he got back into the car.

"The problem with our sister," he told me one day as we were drinking root beer at a gas station outside Salt Lake City, "is that she doesn't know what to do with what she knows." Darienne and Mrs. Silver and my mother were across the road sitting on a fence. Lawrence leaned over and picked a leaf from a patch of iceplant that was growing along the station lot. "Take this iceplant," he said. "Now, what would Dary say about it? That it's the color of the sea or something." He looked at me. "But what would you say about it?"

"That it's a succulent and stores water."

"That's right."

That night we drove until dawn. Darienne and my mother and Mrs. Silver slept in the back while I sat in front with Lawrence. The Great Salt Lake lay somewhere to the side of us, and I watched for it in the moonlight but could not tell it from the salt flats that extended everywhere around, gray and white and as unbroken as lake water. The mountains were gone by early morning. Then mesas appeared, and canyonland, and the road began to climb and dip. Behind us the sky was whitening. Lawrence quizzed me on the motorcycle engine. Then we were silent, the wheels clicking over the expansion fissures in the road.

He turned to me. "Knowledge is power," he said.

"I know."

"I'm going to go out and get that power." He tapped the wheel a couple of times. "I'm going out to California."

He hadn't ever mentioned leaving before. I looked over at him; "That's it," I said. "That's what you were going to tell me."

"Nope."

In fact, he had left Point Bluff once, a few years earlier. But it was only for the summer, when he went to work in Chicago. That was the only time he had ever been gone. He came home once or twice a month. One weekend when he didn't come home he had invited Darienne and me to come see him. He wrote that he would take Darienne to one of the world's great art museums and me to the Cubs game, but my mother wouldn't let us go. She said she didn't trust Chicago. "The Bible has spoken of such cities," she said. "If he wants to see you, he can come back here." He stayed away three months.

"When are you going to be back?"

"I'm going to stay out there a while," he said. "I'm getting into computers. I haven't told anybody yet, Edgar."

"Where will you go?"

"Silicon Valley," he said. "You ought to see it."

"You going to stay out there forever?"

"I'll be back."

"When?"

He sprayed the windshield three times with the automatic washer, then ran the wiper. "Edgar," he said. "You're not thinking about what's important."

I looked ahead of us. There were mobile homes scattered at the roadside. I never knew exactly what he meant when he said that. I tried to think what a twenty-seven-year-old would be thinking. "Are you meeting a girl?"

"Nope."

We drove on. Now the road was jet black in front of us, new asphalt. It was going underneath without noise. I thought about him leaving. Twenty-seven was old to be living in the basement, but I'd had the feeling now for a while that our family was different from other families. Other families we knew went to lakes in the summer. They threw wedding parties. It didn't seem that anybody in our family could ever get married. It didn't seem that anybody could leave.

"Computers are hot," I said.

"That's right."

"And you're good at them."

"I'm great at them."

"Lawrence," I said, "what's Mom going to do?"

He turned around and looked at the three of them asleep in the back. Then he looked straight ahead over the wheel again.

He lowered his voice. "If I told you something, would you keep it quiet?"

I nodded.

He motioned his head toward the back seat. "I don't care what Mom does."

"What?"

He stared ahead.

"What?" I said again. I looked at him sitting next to me. He had the half-Indian nose Darienne gave my father in her paintings. Underneath it his stubble was unclipped. His skin was pocked from old acne. I tried to think, I tried to think *hard*, whether I cared about my mother. Then I looked up. "You sound like a bastard," I said.

He turned to me. "Bingo," he said. He clapped his hands together under the wheel. "That's something important. I *am* a bastard."

I picked my fingernails.

"That's not what I was going to tell you, though." He pointed to his head. "But at least you're thinking. I'll tell you something else, though, right now."

"What is it?"

He held the wheel with his knees and put his arms behind his head. Then he glanced behind us. "I slept with Mrs. Silver," he said.

"What?"

He put his hands back on the wheel and whistled the opening of the Bellini oboe concerto. I looked behind us.

"You did not."

"I sure did. In the basement."

For some reason, although it had nothing to do with Mrs. Silver, I thought again about whether I really cared about my mother. Then I thought about whether I really cared about anybody. Then I thought about Mrs. Silver. I put my arm across the seatback. "Did you really?"

"Women are afraid of getting old," he said.

"So?"

"So, you play on that."

I tried to look behind us again without turning my neck.

Mrs. Silver was asleep with her head leaning back over the seat. Her mouth was open and I saw her throat. She was married to a drunk. I knew that much. I also knew that her husband had been in prison. I paused while we passed some telephone poles. "That's what you were going to tell me, isn't it?"

"Nope."

I couldn't imagine what could be more important than that. Mrs. Silver's throat was white as bath soap, and she was in our house practically every day. When she waxed her legs they shone like my polished clutch plates. I looked at the road and tried to think of what it was like. I imagined waking up one night in my room to find her at the side of my bed, whispering. "Edgar," she would say. Her voice would be low and soft. "Edgar, I can't resist." At a party that year I had felt the breasts of a girl two grades ahead of me.

That afternoon Lawrence and I were in a gas station bathroom. We were drying our hands under the heat fan. "Lawrence," I said. I rubbed my hands together a few times. "Did *she* ask *you?*"

"Did who ask me?"

"You know," I said. The dryer stopped and I put my hands in my pockets. "Did Mrs. Silver ask *you?*"

"In a way."

"In what way?"

"In the way women ask for a thing."

"How do women ask for a thing?"

He walked out to the parking lot and I followed him. We were in the desert. The tar was soft under my shoes, and Darienne and my mother and Mrs. Silver sat on towels on the car hood. Mrs. Silver was wearing a halter top tied high over her abdomen. "They ask for a thing by making you think of it," said Lawrence.

When we got home from our trip that year I started my diary. I hadn't written anything in it before. It was leatherette, with my initials embossed, and it locked. The key was attached by a piece of yellow string. I opened it and reread the inscription. Then I turned to the first page.

JUNE 21st—

I wrote.

LAWRENCE IS LEAVING.

I thought of writing about Mrs. Silver. I closed the diary and locked it, then got a paper clip from the desk. When I tried it, the paper clip opened the lock. I decided not to write about her.

Darienne knocked on the door and came in. "I have to tell you something," she said. She looked at my desk. "You're using that," she said.

"What did you have to tell me?"

"That you can't tell anybody about the cyanide." She stepped behind me. "And you can't write about it, either."

"Why not?"

"It's not even cyanide," she said. "It's a diet pill. You wrote about it, didn't you?"

"Maybe."

"Let me see."

I closed the diary and locked it. She took two oboe reeds from her shirt pocket and put them in her mouth. "You ought to wash those first," I said.

"I knew you'd already written about it."

"I have not. And what do you care if I did?"

"I don't want Lawrence to know. I want him to remember good things about me."

"What if he does know? He knows everything else about you."

"He does not."

"It doesn't matter," I said.

"It does so."

I looked at her. There was always something about her that made me angry. I didn't know what it was. She looked at me as if I were about to hit her. I turned and faced right into her eyes. "It doesn't matter," I said, "because he hates you anyway."

She stepped back and felt for the door handle, and for a

moment I thought she was actually going to fall. Then she left, and I didn't see her again until that afternoon, when she came outside to the yard. Lawrence and I were patching the muffler. She stood off to the side of us, humming the Bellini concerto. Even when she hummed, she repeated parts, went over and over bars as if she were practicing. It was a warm afternoon and I didn't want anything to bother me. I was cutting squares of fiberglass mesh to fit the rust holes in the tailpipe. Lawrence was mixing the hardener. Darienne stopped and repeated a phrase. Then she repeated it again, louder.

"Hi, Dary," I said.

"Hi, Edgar. Hi, Lawrence."

"You're crossing railroad tracks," Lawrence said.

"What?" said Darienne.

"You're crossing a set of railroad tracks," he said, "when the car you're driving stalls." He squeezed out a ribbon of fiberglass putty onto the plastic spatula and mixed it with hardener. Darienne had stopped humming. "You look up and see that around the bend the locomotive is coming. You're right in the middle of the track and the engineer won't see you in time to stop." He picked up the mixture with a spreader and pressed it into the dent in the rear of the tailpipe. "What are you going to do?"

"Start the car," said Darienne.

"It won't start."

"Give it gas."

"It still won't start. The train is coming," he said. He looked at me.

I cut four neat corners on a square of mesh "Get out of the car," I answered.

"Bingo," said Lawrence.

Darienne took a step toward us, reached with her leg, and kicked our parts tray upside down. "You'll never get a job with that hand," she said.

Lawrence laughed. "What did you say?"

"It's a beautiful day out here," I said.

"I said you'll never get a job with that hand of yours."

Lawrence turned around in his crouch. "Damn you," he

whispered. He gathered up a couple of bolts that had rolled next to him. Then he picked up a hammer from the tool chest. So quickly that it seemed to be done by someone else, not by any of us, but by a fourth, by another person, he grabbed Darienne and threw her to the ground. She hit hard on her hip. She was alongside the motorcycle, on her side in the dirt, and he raised the hammer over her face. For a moment its shiny head was above us. My brother's arm was cocked back, stiff with anger. I watched it. I saw the hair and the sweat on his wrist. I saw the hammer's rubber handle and the red steel of its shaft. AMERICAN BEAUTY HARDWARE, it said. The words were printed on aluminum tape wrapped at the neck. There was a rose emblem, black and silver, at the top. At the height of his swing it reflected brilliant light. I didn't say anything. I stood behind them. Darienne screamed. I stepped forward and grabbed Lawrence's hand.

His arm relaxed, and while Darienne scrambled up beside him he let the hammer fall from his grip. Darienne stood. Her skirt was marked with dust and oil. She brushed her cheeks, first one, then the other. Then she turned around and ran into the house.

I turned the parts tray over and began picking up springs and bolts. "Jesus, Lawrence," I said.

"She'll get over it."

In front of me, in the pan, bits of dust floated on the oil. "But you wouldn't have hit her."

"Probably not."

"You can't hit somebody like that." I looked up at him and smiled. "Come on."

He picked up the hammer and put it back in the toolbox. "What the hell would you know about anything?" he said.

We brought Lawrence to the bus station the week before baseball camp started. He left Darienne's painting behind because, he said, he would be back to get it. After breakfast we hung it in the living room. Lawrence said good-bye to Caramel and we got into my mother's Dodge and drove to the station.

When the bus came I helped him on with his stuff. The driver put his duffel underneath and I carried his small suitcase, which had been our father's, into the coach for him. The bus was blue inside and smelled of smoke. It didn't have a skylight. Lawrence took a seat toward the back, next to a middle-aged woman. The driver got back in. I could see Darienne and my mother waiting at the front door. Lawrence went up the aisle and kissed my mother. I watched Darienne let him kiss her also. I got out.

When the bus started to move my mother held Darienne's arm.

"When will he be back?" asked Darienne.

"He walked in all the ways of his father," said my mother.

"Dary, you're not thinking about what's important," I said.

We watched the bus go out to the highway before we got back in our car. On the ride home we stopped for ice cream cones. That evening Mrs. Silver came over and drank vodka cranberries with my mother in the backyard. I drank one too, without ice, and it made me a little drunk. Darienne stayed inside.

I sat on an aluminum chair, my hands tingling from the liquor, and thought of a time when I would barely remember my brother. He would be in California in two days. Then, for as long as I could imagine, I would be living in this house with my mother and my sister. I knew I would never finish the motorcycle. It would lie out in the yard and the rust would eventually enter the engine. But that didn't bother me. I looked at my mother. She was stirring the ice in her glass. Darienne was probably upstairs drawing one line and then another, changing the shading, changing the edge. The light was fading. It seemed to me that all of them, she and my mother and Lawrence, had suffered a wound that had somehow skipped over me. I drank more of my vodka cranberry. Life seemed okay to me. It seemed okay even now, the day my brother left. It even seemed pleasant, which was the way, despite everything she said, I thought it probably seemed to Mrs. Silver.

I looked at her. She was leaning back on a lounger, reading the newspaper. She didn't seem upset about Lawrence leaving. But that's what I would have expected. She wasn't like my mother, and she wasn't like Darienne or Lawrence. Life just flowed over her. It melted over her like wax. I wondered if she cared about anybody. She looked up at me then, as I sat watching her, and I saw that her mouth was rimmed with cranberry.

I smiled. She smiled back. I stood up and went into the house, and after I looked at our new painting for a while I walked upstairs to see my sister. When I came into her room the lights were off except for the Bambi nightlight. It lit the baseboard. In its small, yellow glow I could see Darienne on the bed. Her white legs were drawn up against her chest and she was crying. I went over and sat next to her.

"Hi, Dary."

She didn't say anything. We sat there for a while. She rocked up and back against the wall.

"You shouldn't be so sad," I said. "He was a pecker to you."

"I don't care."

We sat for a few minutes. I thought about things. Then I leaned back next to her. "Dary," I said, "you are driving on a very hot day." I could smell the herbal shampoo in her hair. "A day in which it is over one hundred degrees outside, when you notice halfway up a mountain grade that the temperature gauge on the dashboard indicates hot." I got up from the bed, took a couple of steps across the room, came back. I picked the dirt from my fingernails. "What are you going to do?"

"Edgar, I'm your older sister."

"Come on."

She pulled her knees up.

"The car is overheating."

"I don't know what to do," she said.

I sat lower on the bed again. The two of us pushed together on the quilt. Then, next to her, I started to cry too. I was thinking of Lawrence. Last night I had gone down to his apartment to see him. I almost never went in there. The computer was in a box and his clothes were folded in stacks on the bed. The door was open and the sun was setting, so we went and stood together on the steps. He picked up pebbles from his entranceway and threw them into the yard.

"Have a good time," I said.

"I will."

"When will you visit?"

"I may not be back for a while," he said.

"Not for a while."

"That's right."

"I'll finish the Honda."

"Good."

Then Darienne came down from the house. She walked past Lawrence and stood between us. "I have something to ask you, Edgar," she said.

"What is it?"

"I want to know whether he was going to hit me."

I laughed. I looked at Lawrence's back.

"Tell me," she said.

I laughed again. "Were you going to hit her?" I said to Lawrence.

"I asked *you*," said Darienne.

"You can't ask me that, Dary," I said. "You can't just ask me whether another person was going to do something." I put my hand on her arm.

"Tell me," she said.

"Dary, I can't tell you that. I can tell you what *I* would have done." I leaned down and picked up a couple of pebbles. "But Dary, you knocked over our parts. They're covered with dirt now. There's gravel in the transmission. I can't tell you what Lawrence would or wouldn't do."

"Would he have hit me?"

"I can't tell you that."

Lawrence tossed a pebble over the hedge. "Tell her what you think," he said.

She looked into my eyes. I wanted to change the subject but I couldn't think of anything to say. I smiled. I really tried to think about it. "Yes," I said. "I think he would have."

Darienne turned and went back into the house. I stayed behind Lawrence. Even from the back I thought he was smiling. I threw the pebbles in my palm one by one over the hedge.

"Do you think *you* would have hit her?" he said. He didn't turn around.

"No," I answered.

He chuckled. I thought he was going to say something more,

but he didn't. He let the pebbles drop from his hand.

"You know what I'm waiting for?" I asked.

"You're waiting for me to tell you what I was going to tell you."

"That's right."

"Well," he said. "This is it." He turned around and faced me. "You're a bastard, too," he said.

"What?"

"I mean, yes, you would have hit her too. You just don't know it yet." He pointed at me. "But if something ever goes wrong, you're going to turn into a son of a bitch, just like me." He smiled slightly. "Just like every guy in the world. You don't know it yet because everything's all right so far. You think you're a nice guy and that everything hasn't really affected you. But you can't get away from it." He tapped his chest. "It's in your blood."

"That's what you were going to tell me?"

"Bingo," he said.

Then he brushed past me and went into his apartment. I followed and stood behind him in the doorway. A wind had come up and I put my hands into my pockets. He stood with his back to me, placing shirts into a box, not saying anything. He was wearing a jean jacket and chino pants with pleats. We were silent, standing in his darkening apartment, and I tried to imagine what the world was like for him.

Ethan Canin is the winner of a Houghton Mifflin Literary Fellowship, a James Michener Award, an Iowa Teaching/Writing Fellowship and the Henfield/Transatlantic Review Award. In addition to his own collection, his stories appear in magazines and a number of anthologies. Many of the stories are set in California where he grew up. There is richness, precision and humor in his writing. Ethan Canin is also pursuing a medical career.

For readers who can't read...

Greek, Arabic, Chinese, Japanese, Dutch, Norwegian, Chukchi, Finnish, Hindi, Turkish, Urdu, Hebrew, Russian, Vietnamese, Portuguese, etc., etc.

Short Story International takes you to all points of the compass, to anywhere in the world. There are intriguing stories waiting for you in future issues of SSI—stories that will involve you in corners of this world you've never seen...and in worlds outside this one...with glimpses into the future as well as the past, revealing fascinating, universal truths that bypass differences in language and point up similarities in people.

Send in the coupon below and every other month SSI will take you on a world cruise via the best short stories being published throughout the world today—the best entertainment gleaned from the work of the great creative writers who are enhancing the oldest expression of the entertainment arts—the short story.

A Harvest of the World's
Best Contemporary Writing Selected
and Published Every Other Month

Please enter my subscription to
Short Story International
P.O. Box 405, Great Neck, New York 11022
Six Issues for $24, U.S. & U.S. Possessions
Canada $27 (US), All Other Countries $29 (US)
Enclosed is my check for $ _____ for _____ subscriptions.

Name _____

Address _____

City _____ State _____ Zip _____

Country _____

Please check ☐ *New Subscription* ☐ *Renewal*

Gift for:
Name ——————————————————————————————————
Address ————————————————————————————————
City ————————————————————————State———————— Zip————
Country ————————————————————————————————
Please check □ New Subscription   □ Renewal

Gift for:
Name ——————————————————————————————————
Address ————————————————————————————————
City ————————————————————————State———————— Zip————
Country ————————————————————————————————
Please check □ New Subscription   □ Renewal

Gift for:
Name ——————————————————————————————————
Address ————————————————————————————————
City ————————————————————————State———————— Zip————
Country ————————————————————————————————
Please check □ New Subscription   □ Renewal

Gift for:
Name ——————————————————————————————————
Address ————————————————————————————————
City ————————————————————————State———————— Zip————
Country ————————————————————————————————
Please check □ New Subscription   □ Renewal

Gift for:
Name ——————————————————————————————————
Address ————————————————————————————————
City ————————————————————————State———————— Zip————
Country ————————————————————————————————
Please check □ New Subscription   □ Renewal

Gift for:
Name ——————————————————————————————————
Address ————————————————————————————————
City ————————————————————————State———————— Zip————
Country ————————————————————————————————
Please check □ New Subscription   □ Renewal

For the young people in your life...

The world of the short story for young people is inviting, exciting, rich in culture and tradition of near and far corners of the earth. You hold the key to this world...a world you can unlock for the young in your life...and inspire in them a genuine love for reading. We can think of few things which will give them as much lifelong pleasure as the habit of reading.

Seedling Series is directed to elementary readers (grades 4-7), and **Student Series** is geared to junior and senior high school readers.

Our stories from all lands are carefully selected to promote and strengthen the reading habit.

Give a Harvest of the World's Best Short Stories Published Four Times a Year for Growing Minds.

Please enter my subscription(s) to:

_____ **Seedling Series: Short Story International**
$16 U.S. & U.S. Possessions
Canada $19 (U.S.) All Other Countries $21 (U.S.)

_____ **Student Series: Short Story International**
$18 U.S. & U.S. Possessions
Canada $21 (U.S.) All Other Countries $23 (U.S.)

Mail with check to:
Short Story International
P.O. Box 405, Great Neck, New York 11022
Donor: Name_____
Address_____
City_____ State _____ Zip_____
Country _____

Send To: Name _____
Address _____
City_____ State _____ Zip_____
Country _____
Please check   ☐ *New Subscription*   ☐ *Renewal*

Send To: Name _____
Address _____
City_____ State _____ Zip_____
Country _____
Please check   ☐ *New Subscription*   ☐ *Renewal*